HER VAMPIRE'S PROMISE

JORDAN K. ROSE

This book is a work of fiction. The names, characters, places and incidents are products of the writer's imagination or have been used fictitiously and are not to be construed as real. Any resemblance to persons, living or dead, actual events, locale or organizations is entirely coincidental.

Jordan K. Rose, Publisher
PO Box 714
West Kingston, RI 02892

Her Vampire's Promise
Jordan K. Rose

ISBN: 978-0-9960847-6-5
Ebook ISBN: 978-0-9960847-1-0

Cover design by Robin Ludwig Design Inc.
www.gobookcoverdesign.com

Editors: Judith Roth and Jane Haertel

Jordan K. Rose Publishing August 2014

Her Vampire's Promise

PROLOGUE

Sweat poured from Reade's head, soaking his singed hair. Raging heat scorched the clothes from his body and burned straight to his skin. "Lawrence! Lawrence!" he shouted into the roaring fire.

Whoosh! Flames shot out from the laboratory door, flashing up the walls and over the ceiling. Tumbling backward to the ground, Reade screamed in pain.

For the briefest of moments he wondered if the pain would have been the same if he were still human, or would he already be dead.

Blisters bubbled over his arms and chest, a searing ripple tore down his back like a hot razor blade slicing his skin, but he crawled toward the door. He wouldn't leave without them. He'd never leave them. "Lawrie. Baby girl." He strained to hear their voices—a call for help from his old scientist friend or a cry from the toddler he'd come to love as his own.

"Reade! Reade, no!" someone hollered behind him.

He kept going, climbing over fallen beams and crackling cinders. There was no way he'd let them perish. Not after all that had happened, not after the connection, the bond they had to each other. He would not give up. He would die trying.

Reaching the doorway, he dragged himself over the threshold, feeling the flesh of his abdomen and then his thighs rip away, but still he moved further into the chamber, searching for any sign of life.

"Lawrie! Lawrie!" He howled into the inferno that engulfed the laboratory where the baby slept while her father worked at his experiments. "Lawrie, please…" his voice choked when he peered into the corner to find the crib devoured in a ball of deadly flames.

"Reade, we have to get out of here." Someone grabbed his legs and pulled him back toward the door.

"No! Not without them. Not without Lawrie." His fingers dug into the melting linoleum, leaving deep grooves as he was dragged back from the last place he saw them both alive. He kicked and swung blindly at whoever had grabbed him.

"It's too late! They're gone." The words cut like knives driven into his heart.

"No. It's not true. I would know." He struggled to free himself, but someone else joined in the fight to make him leave. "I would know. If she hadn't made it, I would know."

The pain of breaking a blood bond was worse than a quick death, worse than a long and tortured death. It was the same as having your own soul ripped from your body.

"I would know." The sound of his voice, like a sob of defeat spurred him to keep fighting.

Sitting up, he shoved out of the grip of whoever had him and tumbled over, quickly finding it impossible to hold his own weight. His body was too badly burned, and he'd lost far too much blood.

"We have a blood bond. I would know." Tears leaked from the corners of his eyes as he rocked on the floor, realizing he was not strong enough to do any more.

He had a bond with that little girl that went far deeper than any other he'd felt, a blood bond that bound them together forever. For the rest of his existence he'd feel her loss deep in his soul.

"They're gone. Anyone who hasn't made it out at this point is gone," a familiar voice said as Reade was slung over someone's shoulder. "We have to go."

Looking back at the laboratory, where smoke unfurled from a brilliant fiery wall, Reade's heart crumbled. He had lived and Lawrie was gone.

"Leave me. Let me die," he begged, waiting for his soul to writhe in the agony of its loss.

"There will be no death for you tonight."

Chapter One

TWENTY YEARS LATER.

Reade wished he'd thought twice about returning to this dump. The stale stink of cigarettes clinging to the walls and furniture assaulted him the moment he opened the door. He'd known better than to agree to take the assignment with Garrison, but curiosity had him crawling back for more. And here he sat in the same dingy bar where he'd wasted many a night in Central City.

"Make fun of me because I'm not as smart as them. We'll see who has the last laugh." The woman sitting on the barstool beside him shook her head. "Jackasses."

He watched the bartender refill his shot glass. Maybe it wasn't curiosity. If he were honest with himself, he'd have to admit it was the idea of having one more chance at vengeance. Twenty years was a long time to wait. It was a long time to think about what he'd do if opportunity came knocking.

"When my moment comes, they'll rue the day they laughed." She snatched a handful of nuts from the bowl in front of her. "Then the tables will turn. Then they'll see who's the dog."

He'd been warned about coming back here. Nothing good ever came out of Central City anymore. That's what he'd been told. But the warning didn't stop him. He had to come. He'd do anything for one more chance to make it right.

"Treat me like I'm stupid. Act like I can't possibly understand basic chemistry. I know the periodic table." She smashed her fist onto the bar, cracking open the peanut shell.

In the last several weeks the desire to have his revenge burned hotter than it had in two decades. It festered deep in his gut, burning and screaming for release. He hadn't felt this much angst since the incident.

"And I'm not afraid. Wait. Just wait until they learn what I've done." She picked the peanuts out of the shell. "Then they'll be sorry."

He wished he hadn't sat beside the pretty blonde. Problem was he'd always been a sucker for long hair and big boobs.

But even his two favorite attributes couldn't make up for her nonstop bitching.

"Huh, tell me I'm not good enough. They told me I'm

not one of them. They said I don't belong." She sucked hard on her straw once again, swallowing the last mouthful in her glass. "I'm smart enough. Smarter than they know. I've memorized things. Important things. I'll show them."

If the bartender would turn around from the ball game on the television, he'd be more than happy to buy her another fruity concoction. Maybe it would keep her quiet for five damn minutes.

Why had Garrison picked this dump? The guy always loved the crummiest places. It wasn't as if meeting in the coffee shop down the street wouldn't have worked. He was certain there was only one person left in Central City who'd recognize them, and that person rarely left Panthera.

There had been talk of something happening at Panthera. New buildings being built. Production facilities ramping up. Possibly a state of the art laboratory. The company hadn't produced anything worthwhile since one of the cofounders was killed in the explosion all those long years ago. If there was action now, Reade knew it was not to his benefit.

Staking out Panthera was the perfect job for him.

"I'm not good enough? I'm just as good as any of them." She slapped her hand onto the counter top, then crossed her arms over her chest. "I'm not afraid. I'm not the one who hypothesizes but doesn't act. I'll show them. When I'm through, they'll never doubt me again."

Her foot tapped furiously against the leg of his

barstool. The rapid banging was beginning to annoy him more than her babbling.

"Family first? Oh, well, that all depends on how you define family. With a family like this, who needs enemies?"

He pushed his seat over a couple inches.

Her head snapped to the right. "What? I'm not good enough for you either?"

Reade shook his head and didn't bother to look in her direction. No sense in fueling her ire. "You can't pick your family." When he raised his shot glass to his lips the smell of very cheap whiskey assailed his nostrils, and he knew what he was about to taste wasn't what he'd ordered.

"No, but the smart ones get away." She stared into her empty mug. The remaining few drops of her red girly drink pooled in the bottom, too small an amount for her to suck up into the straw, though he enjoyed watching her try. "They escape. The rest of us die slow deaths."

The turpentine burn of cheap whiskey roared down Reade's throat. "You should be glad to have family. Some of us have none." He replaced the glass on the bar and contemplated leaping over to thank the bartender for serving him swill. He could easily make his point without worry of being caught.

Being one of only two patrons inside the dive, and noting no security cameras, he was certain no one would ever notice. It would be a breeze to make his point and have a little sip of the man without anyone in the establishment being able to tell a soul. God knew the woman beside him was too obsessed with her own misery to notice anything else.

"The lucky ones." She flicked her straw onto the bar.

Reade sat back. She might have a point, though he certainly did miss his mother. He'd had little to no use for his father or his older brothers, who'd been raised to be as cruel as the old man.

His mother, now, she had been a saint. He still remembered the sound of her voice so clearly and the way her smile reached all the way into her eyes. Yeah, he missed his mom.

The woman beside him huffed. "Assholes." Her voice muffled into her glass as she tipped her head back, letting the last few drops of her sugary drink roll into her mouth.

He watched her long neck swallow and felt an ache in his gut. He hadn't fed tonight. In fact, he hadn't fed in two nights. Without realizing he swallowed along with her.

Despite her incessant babbling, something about her intrigued him. Her scent was familiar, though he was certain he hadn't encountered her before. The pretty little crazy ones were impossible to forget. They were the ones who sparked his interest.

She banged her mug onto the bar and waved the bartender over. "Mic, I'll have another."

The bald man glanced over his shoulder, turning his head so slowly Reade wondered if he'd ever stop. He gave her an almost unnoticeable nod and headed to the blender.

"Make sure you add the liquor this time." She snickered

at the tattooed Neanderthal. "Cheap bastard. Always trying to cheat the customer. Like I need to be jerked around by him, too."

The bartender shook his head. "You're the one who ordered the virgin daiquiri."

Reade chuckled.

"What are you laughing at?" She gave him a sideways glance, her pale blue eyes narrowing to slits. "You laughing at me, too?" She turned to face him, resting one hand on the bar.

Her right hand balled to a fist, and she clenched her jaw.

Reade couldn't help but smile. She'd said she was pissed. She'd spent the last twenty minutes ranting about why. She'd been very clear about wanting to smash someone. The little thing wanted her fight, and she was willing to have it with anyone.

But a fight was not part of his plan tonight, least of all with a woman.

"I've had just about all I'm going to take of being laughed at today. So, unless you want me to move that stupid grin to the back of your head, I suggest you lose it." She leaned forward, one hand gripping the bar hard enough to turn her fingers white. The other hand curled so tightly her nails had to be cutting into her palms.

The pungent scent of anger perfumed the air. Anger and blood.

Reade shook his head. The poor girl was just aching for

a chance to unleash a world of pent-up rage. She was so consumed by her anger she couldn't possibly be thinking straight.

What woman challenged a man twice her size, a stranger even, and never mind the fact that he was a more lethal predator than she could possibly know?

If she held a gun in her hand, she still stood no chance against him. With vampire speed and the ability to seduce any woman or man he had no worries. He hadn't lost a fight in years, decades, quite possibly two centuries.

His gaze dropped from her face. With her chest puffed up her boobs stood out nicely. He guessed her size to be a full C cup, if not a D. His mouth watered. What he wouldn't like to do to her. The possibilities were endless.

"That's it." She jumped up from her seat. "You were warned."

Reade saw the blur of her hand. He even noticed the lion's head carved in her ring before it made contact with his nose. The fact he was lying flat on his back on the barroom floor was less surprising than the echoing sound of bones crunching under the power of her little fist. His ears rang with that awful noise.

"Ow!" He grabbed his nose, pressing fingers on either side and forcing it back into a straight line. "What the hell are you doing, woman?"

Chapter Two

"Nobody laughs at me. Nobody." Lawrie stood over the jerk, hands at her sides, wiggling her fingers. They itched for another chance to hit him. The next time she'd knock his lights out.

She felt strong, a tad bit out of control, and angry. Her senses were much more heightened than usual. Her heart beat like a battle drum. Blood zoomed through her veins. It was exhilarating. For once she was powerful.

How dare this stranger mock her? Hadn't she suffered enough indignity? Wasn't she entitled to a moment's peace? She'd come to the most remote establishment she knew, the one she always hid in, not to be laughed at, but to relax and focus on herself and anything that might seem different, to be able to sit in a place where she didn't have to hide for fear someone would make fun of her inadequacies and yell out that she was an idiot, a useless dolt.

Her hand ached a bit, not much, but it did hurt a little. She'd never hit anyone before. In fact, she'd never lifted a finger to anyone. Generally, she wasn't a violent person. In all truthfulness most of the time she shied away from confrontation as it never seemed to end well. At least that was her experience. It never ended well for her. But tonight was different, very different.

She felt strong, confident, indestructible. She wasn't taking crap from anyone, least of all some stranger who didn't know her and had no right to shun her.

"You broke my nose." His deep voice was much more nasally than before. He sounded ridiculous. Several locks of chestnut-colored hair flopped into his face.

Lawrie snarled. "Jerk."

Blood dripped down his chin as he cradled his nose.

Anger shown in his dark eyes, more like anger-filled hatred. That look had appeared many times before and on several faces. She hadn't deserved it then and she didn't deserve it now.

Sprawled on the floor, she couldn't quite tell his height, but he was certainly large, larger than she'd realized when he was seated beside her. His shoulders were easily twice as wide as hers, maybe wider.

The top few buttons of his blue shirt had popped off, leaving a clear view of his hard chest. The fabric of the sleeves stretched tightly around his biceps. Dear God, his muscles were enormous. His arms had to be three times as thick as her spaghetti limbs.

"You laughed at me." She repositioned herself, stepping back a few inches to give herself room. Bringing her arms up in front, dukes ready to attack, just as she'd seen her cousins do when they fought, she waited.

Barely able to control herself, her body hummed with energy. Anticipation. Excitement. The thrill of not being afraid pulsed within her.

When the man sat up every muscle from his chest to his waist flexed. His glare never left her face. Deep within his eyes something lethal prowled. She sensed a part of him waiting to be set loose, waiting to spring.

Experimenting on herself might not have been the best idea. Clearly it had caused her to suffer impaired decision-making skills, not to mention her language was more vulgar than usual.

The man's head dipped low, his stare remaining deadly. Lawrie knew that when he stood, if he took a swing at her, no matter how much RH+ she'd taken, she was dead.

Rocking back and forth, she kept the bar to her back and her fists at the ready. She would take her next shot. There was no way she would go down without a fight.

He scrambled to his feet, backing away from her and protecting his face. "Being laughed at is no reason to break my nose." He scowled at her, though with the now disheveled clothes, nasally voice, and defensive posture he wasn't nearly as scary.

"Where I'm from we don't take kindly to being laughed at." That was an understatement. Anyone foolish enough to laugh at her uncle or cousins never did it twice. In fact, she wondered if they ever did anything again.

"Is that so?" He angled toward her.

He might have been right. She probably shouldn't have slugged him. Normal people, normal, well-mannered people who had been raised in a family who loved them didn't hit strangers in bars for laughing. But, she wasn't raised to be well mannered. The truth of the matter was she'd practically raised herself.

"Where I'm from ladies don't pick fights." He swiped his hair out of his face. His eyes were the darkest blue she'd ever seen, darker than his jeans, and no longer filled with anger. Now he simply appeared in pain. He pinched the bridge of his nose.

Maybe she had overreacted to his smile. But she was clearly running on instinct. Instinct and RH+, which might be why her instinct was running amuck.

Nonetheless, she couldn't help how her instinct reacted. They'd driven her to it. They'd made her crazy with the incessant bickering and the constant insults. She'd become a product of her environment.

This was a thought she needed to catalogue. Was there a difference in how a specimen would react to RH+ based on that specimen's upbringing or current state of physical, emotional, or mental well-being?

It was only logical to assume the answer would be yes, however, a good scientist would test this theory. How would someone raised in a loving family with people who genuinely cared for her react to RH+? Lawrie had no idea nor did she know how she'd test that question.

If she had more, could she simply slip the RH+ into the drink of one of the lab techs? She could start with just a few drops to see if there was any reaction. She thought she recalled overhearing one of them say she loved her mother. Maybe she'd use that woman as a...what was she thinking? She couldn't simply experiment on people without their permission. She wasn't her uncle. She was better than that. She was Lawrence Tyrone's daughter. She had morals. Scruples. She cared.

Once.

The man with the broken nose groaned. "I'd forgotten how much a broken nose hurts."

It was like she needed detox in order to be out in public. Lawrie hated what she'd become. Maybe she should apologize. She frowned. Why was she always the one who had to apologize?

The muscles in his cheek bulged, his jaw set, and he winced as more blood dripped down his chin. "Damn it." He growled and reached toward her.

Survival instincts kicked into high gear.

There was no way he was getting his hands on her. She didn't care if she had been out of line. He shouldn't hit a woman. She could never defend against him. He was too big. As fast and hard as she could she yanked her knee up in one smooth, swift motion.

"Ooow." He doubled over. Not missing a beat she

punched him in his cheek. “Aah.” He landed on his knees, one hand holding his face and the other cupping his groin.

“My hand. Oh, my hand. My hand.” Lawrie bent forward, cradling her hand and whimpering. “Oh, it hurts. It hurts.”

She’d never been in a bar brawl before. Generally speaking, she was a coward. Tonight’s events were a bit out of character. She’d make a note of that fact when summarizing her experiment, assuming she lived through the night and remained human.

That was just one other potential side effect she’d chosen not to focus on earlier, though it probably should have been more of a consideration before taking the RH+.

“Why does it hurt so much?” She dropped onto the floor beside the man she’d just beaten, unable to bring herself to look at her hand. She thought for sure it was crushed. “Oooh.”

“Lawrie, have you never seen a real fight?” The bartender leaned over the bar to stare down. “A real fight is much uglier and a lot more painful than in the movies.” He lowered a bag of ice cubes. “Here, buddy. This might help your balls.”

The man reached up from the floor where he’d curled into the fetal position still clutching the family jewels. Faster than Lawrie could register, the bag of ice disappeared between his legs.

“What is your fucking problem, woman?” He glared at

her. "In all my years I've never met a woman who picked fights with strangers."

"You were coming at me," she snapped. "What did you think, I'd just stand there and let you hit me? I wasn't letting you get the drop on me." Taking the bag of ice now offered her, she tried to place it on her hand without crying, but she hurt too damn much to keep the tears from leaking.

"You broke my nose. I was bleeding like a bastard." He grunted when another bag of ice was lowered onto his face.

"I know. That's why you were coming for me. Ow. Ow. Ow. You wanted revenge."

"Bloody hell! I wanted a napkin to stop the bleeding."

Chapter Three

"I'm sorry," the psycho blonde mumbled.

"As you should be." Reade opened his eyes to see her kneeling beside him, giant tears rolling down her face and a bag of ice resting on top of her hand, the one he was sure she'd broken on his cheekbone.

Swallowing loudly, she took a deep, shaky breath. When she lifted the ice, her hand trembled. "Oh God." She carefully replaced the bag all the while puffing out quick breaths.

"And what do we have here?" Two red snakeskin boots appeared beside Reade's head. "Looks like someone got the shit kicked out of him *by a girl*." Garrison squatted, bringing his giant grin into Reade's line of vision. "I told you to get a better pickup line."

This was turning out to be the worst night of Reade's life. He had not been in a bar brawl in more years than he could remember. In fact the last one had occurred before he'd left Ireland, which was well before these United States were even penal colonies.

He'd never been beaten by a woman. Never.

More importantly, he'd never been taken by surprise.

That may not have been entirely true. He certainly hadn't seen the vampire coming at him. That was a complete surprise. But other than that one time, he'd never been unaware of a potential attack. Not until tonight.

The little psycho beside him had not only bested him, but she'd pretty much ended any thoughts he had about fucking her or any other woman this evening.

He lay on the floor praying the pain radiating up into his gut would go away and that his balls would stop throbbing so he could get up off the floor.

To make matters worse, Garrison pulled out his phone and took pictures.

"Oh, that's a perfect one to text to the gang. Smile, please." The flash on the camera phone went off.

The only thing Reade could do to console himself was enjoy watching her whimper in pain. He only wished her knee hurt, too.

"If you two can make it up off the floor, the next round is on me." The bartender stared down at them, holding a towel in one hand and a beer glass in the other. "I'll even give you the good stuff." He laughed.

"I knew you'd given me crap." Reade groaned as he tried to raise himself off the floor. "Sewage would taste better."

The bartender laughed again. "Wouldn't know. Never drink sewage."

Garrison hoisted Reade onto his feet. "Man, I wish I'd gotten here sooner."

"You missed a good show," the bartender said. "What'll you have?"

"Whiskey. Neat." Garrison stepped around Lawrie. "The good stuff."

Reade collapsed onto the barstool and repositioned the ice between his legs, hopeful he still had two balls.

"Would you like me to help you up, firecracker?" Garrison asked Lawrie.

"Don't touch me."

"You don't have to tell me twice." Garrison made a show of stepping well around her. "Don't want to become another of your victims."

Lawrie remained on the floor. Her body now shook. Reade surmised she'd never felt that kind of pain. Served her right, though watching her suffer was no longer comforting. He may have been a ruthless bastard, but he wasn't cruel.

"You'd better at least take that ring off before your finger swells." Reade winced and adjusted the bag of ice at his temple, trying to keep his left eye from seeing double.

Nodding, she moved the bag of ice. Her hand was already bruised and swollen, and quite obviously broken in several places. "Oh, my God," she whimpered and gasped. Several quick, shallow breaths followed.

Garrison let out a low whistle. "That's a bad break. Did that happen when she broke your nose or your cheek?"

"My cheek." A sharp jab shot from Reade's left cheekbone straight to the bridge of his nose. His vision was blurry. He tossed back the whiskey in one mouthful. "Pour me another."

Uncontrollable shaking wracked Lawrie's body, and she panted like an overheated puppy.

Reade couldn't bear to watch her. In the last hour he'd wished several things—from her mouth being magically clamped shut to her growing a set of balls that had been permanently kicked inward, but when it came down to it, he'd never had it in him to watch a woman cry, let alone suffer in pain.

He dropped his ice bag from his face and lifted the other from his lap before kneeling beside her. "Let me see it."

She shook her head and tried to move away, but he trapped her where she sat, ensuring she had no leverage to knock him over, no room to pull a punch, and absolutely no use of her knees or feet.

Not wanting to add to her agony, he gently gripped her wrist. When she tried to pull back, he didn't yield. He touched the ring on her middle finger and she winced. On either side of the gold her skin bulged, swelling up and over the mound of string wrapped around the underside of the ring.

"What's with all the string?" He reached into his back pocket and pulled out a switchblade.

"It's too big." She squeezed her eyes shut and rocked back and forth, forcing Reade to tighten his hold on her.

"I see that. Whose was it before you got your hands on it?" Reade slid the tip of the knife along the string, being very careful to keep her hand still. The last thing they needed was for her to start bleeding.

The fact that he hadn't fed in two days, had been beaten by a lovely, though clearly unstable woman and was struggling to heal his own wounds already meant his self-control was teetering on a precarious edge. Adding a free flow of blood to the mix would make it near impossible for him to maintain any amount of civility.

"My dad's." She sniffled.

Reade's entire body tightened. The last time he'd seen this ring it was on the hand of its original owner. A man Reade trusted with his own life.

Lawrie clamped her teeth together and sucked in a long breath. "It's all I have left of him."

He could barely keep from shaking. All these long years of fruitless searching, and Lawrie Tyrone simply appeared at a bar. She smelled so much as she had the last time he held her. If memory served him, and he knew it did for he'd replayed it at least a million times, he was the last one to hold her before her father died.

Reade saw the vision of her sleepy baby face as he laid her in her little pink princess bed. He'd rocked her until she drifted off to sleep.

Lawrie Tyrone was no baby any more.

He gently sliced through the wad of string. "It's a good thing it's so big. It might save you from losing the finger."

Her eyes opened wide. "What?"

"Well, if the ring doesn't come off, I'm betting that finger will." He tugged at the broken string, pulling a few strands free and she hissed. "Loss of circulation usually leads to amputation." After he slipped more string out the ring began to move.

Lawrie's pulse pounded against Reade's fingers. "I can't lose my finger. I…I need it." Her mouth hung open.

He gingerly slid the ring from her finger. "I assume you do, Lawrie." He held it up, studying the inscription. "Nice lion's head. Dad's name was Lawrence?"

She snatched the ring away with her good hand, pocketing it faster than any pickpocket he'd ever met. "Yes. I was named after him." She blew gentle puffs of air at the dented skin where her ring had been.

Garrison sat back on his stool, his attention clearly focused on Lawrie. "So, that's Lawrie with a W, then?" He locked gazes with Reade.

She nodded, still whimpering about her hand.

Reade knew instantly that he and Garrison were wondering the same damn thing. After more than twenty years of searching for Lawrence's heir and having to accept they might never know the truth, how could Lawrie Tyrone simply walk into a bar?

Sweat beaded on her forehead. Her heart continued to beat alarmingly fast.

She sat before him, her mouth open, brows furrowed, pain etching her face.

Reade turned her hand over to look at her knuckles. He was completely perplexed at how such a small hand could break his nose and then his cheekbone, but somehow these dainty little fingers had done just that.

She'd been lucky it wasn't worse. Vampire bones were considerably stronger than human bones, strongest of any creature. How she managed to break his face was perplexing at best and terrifying for sure.

Was it possible that twenty years after the incident she was still experiencing residual side effects? Could there still be cells of vampire blood living inside her?

She seemed to be full of mysteries, sneak attacks, fists of fury, and being the little girl who'd gone missing more than two decades ago, everything about her made him very curious. Where the hell had she been all this time?

"Looks like you broke three knuckles and a finger or two." When he softly squeezed each finger, she inhaled sharply. "Won't be able to use this hand for a bit. I hope you're ambidextrous."

"I'm not." She swiped the back of her other hand at the tears rolling down her cheeks.

"Maybe you should see a doctor," the bartender suggested.

Reade glanced up to find the man leaning over the bar.

She shook her head. "No. I've got to get home."

Trying to stand, but not quite stable on her feet, she stumbled forward.

"Gonna be tough to ride your bike with that hand," the bartender said.

"Easy." Reade caught her and lifted her onto the barstool. "Try your fruity whatever it is." He slid the drink toward her. "Might help calm you, though if I were you, I'd try something a lot stronger." He carefully placed the bag of ice on her hand and downed the shot of whiskey waiting for him before pressing his own bag of ice to his cheek.

"A bike? You rode that thing in here?" Garrison leaned back and looked at the ten-speed propped near the door. "A bike. Don't you own a car?"

She shook her head again.

"Well, at least you won't be a danger on the roadway." Garrison looked her over, then faced forward, watching her in the mirror with the casualness of a centuries-old vampire.

In order to heal his injuries Reade would have to feed. He'd just been reminded of why vampires fed every night. He closed his eyes against the pain in his face. Had he simply fed like he should have, the pain would be far less and his wounds would already be healing.

Instead, he'd been slightly obsessed with replaying the events from twenty years ago, searching for some clue that would help answer the questions of where Lawrie Tyrone had gone and what Raymond had been up to all these years.

This was why he never came to Central City. Whenever he did, he could think of only that night, which inevitably led to bad decisions.

They sat quietly for a few minutes. Reade caught Lawrie peering at him through a curtain of hair. When he watched her in the mirror across from them, he saw she was doing the same thing to Garrison.

If she wasn't looking at either of them she was making a valiant attempt not to hyperventilate each time she looked at her hand.

"Well, seems I was wrong," Garrison said.

"Clearly." Reade motioned for the bartender to fill his glass.

"Who knew?"

"I did." Reade had always known Lawrie was alive. He'd made a solemn promise to Lawrence to protect his little girl, a blood pact.

"I thought you were crazy." Garrison's gaze met his in the mirror.

They'd all thought he was crazy for his constant attempts to get The Guard to consider a rescue mission. He'd been told countless times that she was dead, but he knew differently. He knew the truth because that night he'd sworn to protect her life with his own, and if he was still alive, she had to be.

"Several questions still remain."

Reade nodded.

"The Guard will want details of the last two decades."

Garrison was right. The Guard would be very suspicious and rightfully so. Lawrie had been all of three years old when her father was killed. That was plenty of years for Raymond to program her to be something he wanted, something her father would have hated. Something that could destroy The Guard.

"Their new product has to be something much more potent." Garrison's voice was a deep whisper.

"Agreed." Reade studied Lawrie's face as he listened to Garrison. Though she was clearly in pain she was still quite beautiful.

Her blue eyes looked like glass. Her skin was perfect, pale as his, like she'd never been in the sun. Platinum tresses hung down her back, nearly to her waist. They draped over her breasts like silk. He was back to imagining his mouth on her skin.

She had certainly grown up since the last time he'd seen her. He tried to picture her as the little girl she'd been, the one whose laugh was contagious, even to vampires. But he couldn't seem to conjure that memory with her sitting beside him.

One thing was certain. His balls and his cock had survived her attack. He shifted in his chair.

Garrison's voice brought him out of his thoughts. "Sounds like they might be weeks, possibly days from production."

"Can't let that happen." Reade dropped his other bag of ice into his lap. Might as well cool things now. No sense in letting his imagination get the best of him. That's what landed him in this position.

"This certainly changes things." Garrison smiled. "Can't believe our luck. Could get the exact details tonight."

"Seems odd how our luck always involves me taking one for the team," Reade said, remembering the last time they'd been paired up to do reconnaissance work.

Garrison laughed. "Yeah, well, you're a good front man."

Lawrie turned her chair. "I have to go." She reached for her bike.

Garrison's hand went to the back of her seat, spinning her around to face the bar. His gaze locked with Reade's in the mirror. "This is going to require all your strength. You'll need to do whatever it takes to heal." He nodded toward Lawrie. "A little tit for tat." He smiled.

Reade had twice considered the option of drinking from Lawrie earlier, once when he walked into the joint and saw the beauty sitting alone at the bar and later when she wouldn't shut up. But then he thought better after she'd attacked him the first time, and not because he hadn't wanted to hurt her because God, how he'd wanted to snap her in two.

But having seen the ring's emblem, he knew he needed her alive more than he needed to teach her a lesson.

Lawrie stared into the mirror. Her teary blue eyes blinked at Reade, and he noticed how she nibbled her lip.

Sitting between the two vampires, she appeared smaller and more fragile than before, though he was no longer foolish enough to believe her weak.

The strangest urge to pull her into his arms and care for her wounds, to wipe away her tears and somehow bring a smile to her face flooded Reade's mind. He considered the many ways he'd make her smile.

The ice was proving to be no match for his imagination. He forced his mind to remember the battle that left her father dead. Those images made it quite easy to cool his desire.

"I really should go," Lawrie said to the mirror. Her gaze shifted from Reade to Garrison.

"What's your hurry?" Garrison grinned, and although it was one of his more playful expressions, it was laced with menace. "I'm simply dying to know what my friend did to provoke an ass kicking."

Lawrie turned to Reade. "I apologize. I never should have done that."

Reade raised his eyebrows. "No. You shouldn't." His voice was huskier than before.

"I said I was sorry." She forced the words through gritted teeth, and Reade wasn't sure if it was a display of pain or anger.

"Are you actually irritated with me for not being pleased you've apologized? You attacked me. Twice. I have every right to be angry." He turned sideways to look at her.

Garrison came to stand between them, keeping his

hand on her chair and placing his foot up on the footrest, thus pinning her legs and ensuring both men's nether regions remained safe from attack. "Do you want Reade to forgive you?"

"I…well, I don't plan to ever see him again so I guess I don't honestly care." She tilted her chin up and met Reade's gaze.

"Well, now, that's an honest answer." Garrison chuckled. "But you do owe him."

"What?" She shrugged Garrison's hand off her shoulder. "I apologized. I misunderstood his intent and made a mistake. I don't owe him anything. Well, maybe I could help with his doctor's bill." Her voice cracked, and Reade had the feeling her suggestion worried her.

Garrison shook his head. "He's not seeing a doctor."

"Well, then I'd say we're even." She cleared her throat.

"How do you figure?" Garrison waved the bartender over. "Another round, and bring her a whiskey instead of that girly drink." He narrowed his eyes. "No swill either."

The bartender set a shot glass in front of Lawrie and poured another round.

"I…I…offered to pay…" She looked confused.

Garrison removed the bag of ice from Lawrie's hand and trailed his finger from her wrist up her middle finger and back down. "He saved your finger. Without him you might have lost that middle finger, a finger we all know is very important."

She didn't acknowledge Garrison. Instead she pulled

her hand away and looked at Reade. "What do you want?"

Garrison tilted Lawrie's chin toward him, pinning her with his gaze. "We want Lawrence Tyrone's only living heir to tell us where's she's been for the last twenty years and what's going on at Panthera."

"And she's not leaving here until she does." Reade turned to face the bartender. "Lock the door, then go in the back and wait." The man scurried off to do as he was ordered. When they were finally alone, Reade's attention trained on Lawrie. "Start talking."

Chapter Four

Lawrie's mouth dropped open. How did they know who she was? She had only ever left the compound three times and all three times she'd landed here. She had never shared any information about herself with anyone. Her entire life was a secret, even to her.

"I don't know what you're talking about." She jerked her chin from the tall, lanky stranger's hand.

"Come now. You know exactly what I'm talking about, Lawrie Marie." He curled his lips into what she knew was a fake smile. It appeared about as welcoming as a hyena's. "You are your father's daughter. I'll give you that. Same nose. Same brave heart and stubborn streak. But you probably know that didn't save him. It won't save you either."

Lawrie stiffened in her chair. She'd studied both men, each pale, each with a certain air about him that said he was more than just a man. She was fairly certain they were vampires, though she'd never seen one in person and neither sported a set of giant canines.

They appeared like normal men, but there was something different, something indescribable, yet very clearly present. It was power, confidence, arrogance.

Vampires thought they were impossible to defeat. But everyone had a weak spot.

"Bravery is no defense against treachery," the tall vampire said.

She'd only ever heard that her father's death was due to his own stupidity. Her uncle made it very clear her father was to blame for the botched experiments and the near collapse of Panthera. Lawrence Tyrone was considered a traitor within the company and the family.

She never believed it. She couldn't. Her gut told her he'd been a good man, noble, honorable, kind. Her heart told her he wasn't anything like her uncle. Yet, his notes told her everything about his alliance with the vampires.

Was he a traitor? What she wouldn't give to know the truth about his death. Nearly everything she had, short of her own life.

"If you lay another hand on me, I'll do worse to you than I did to him." She mustered all the anger she had, channeled every bit of the pain from her hand at the tall stranger.

"Do you mean to tell me you're equally as good with your left hand as you are with your right? I don't believe it. That would make you ambidextrous, which you admitted you are not." He stepped back. "Go ahead. Take your best shot." He waved her toward him. "If you insist on this tactic, I'll do battle with you. You must be a worthy adversary, seeing how you defeated one of the best fighters I've ever sparred with."

"Garrison," her first victim said.

"What? I want my chance with her. Wouldn't be right for you to be the only one Lawrence laughs at from his grave." He bowed to her. "We should get this going so that we can get back to business. Time's a-wasting."

Lawrie stood up from her stool, holding onto the bar with her good hand. Her right hand throbbed, and the ache pulsed through her entire body. She feared her knees might give out, but that didn't stop her. She would not go down without a fight.

Garrison was mocking her. The first guy had mocked and now this guy. Where were they from, the land of mockery?

"Reade, you know how he loved a good laugh. Can't imagine he feels any different now." Garrison shrugged his shoulders and cracked his knuckles. "Come little firecracker. Take your best shot."

She hated being treated this way. All her life every man around her treated her as though she was some silly girl to be knocked around and told she was a fool. *You think you understand physics? You don't know a damn thing. You think you understand the chemical engineering of plasma? Stupid girl. Go play with your dolls.*

The brute in front of her waited. His shorn black hair and stubbly chin added to his already terrifying presence. He cocked his head to the side and stood perfectly still.

She snickered. Everyone doubted her, but she *had* understood. She'd learned faster than her cousins. She'd memorized every formula, every flaw, every success and every failure. She knew why the experiments didn't work and what not to try, but they never listened. They never gave her a second thought. *Get back to the stock room. Clean the bins.*

That's all they thought she was good for and now these two idiots thought the same. She wouldn't have been surprised to learn they'd been sent to terrorize her.

Lawrie stepped away from Reade, then took another step back to give herself room.

"Where you going?" Garrison asked.

What if she was right and these two worked for her uncle? What if her uncle knew she'd escaped the compound? The punishment would be far worse than a broken hand.

"Garrison, don't do this. She's in enough pain." Reade turned from his friend to Lawrie. "You don't need to fight him. We just want to talk." Even though what he said wasn't threatening, his tone was completely different. Anger still edged his words. Dried blood formed a crusty line down his chin. "You don't want to have to explain this to your uncle."

How could her uncle have known she'd been coming

here? Had she been followed? Had the bartender given her away? Mic had been the only person she'd told her first name, and she'd never told him where she lived. She even parked her damn bike in the bar so no one would see it outside.

"You don't know what I want or don't want." She squared her shoulders, remembering her father's letters to her. *Always keep your head high and shoulders back when facing an adversary.*

Whether or not her uncle had sent these guys she knew she had to prove herself tonight or die trying. Being dragged back to the compound wounded was not an option. She needed to take care of these two and sneak back to her room. Tomorrow she'd claim she fell on her hand and face the taunts.

"I'm not afraid of him or you."

"Well, there's your first mistake." Garrison stepped toward her, closing the four-foot space between them down to only a foot or two.

Lawrie inched backward. "That's my first mistake? Coming here wouldn't have been my first mistake?"

"No. Coming here was not a mistake. You did that on purpose. You must have had some sort of plan." Garrison's gaze dropped to her right hand. "Something's up and you're just dying to talk. I can see that in your eyes. Suspicion. Excitement. We'll talk to you. We'd love to talk to you."

Shifting her weight and bringing her left foot forward,

she moved her right hand behind her back, out of his reach. "What do you want to talk about?"

"Oh, many things, like your uncle for one. Maybe your father for two." Garrison glanced at Reade, whose veiled expression never changed.

Whether they'd come to torment her or not, they clearly had information she wanted. "Care to make a wager?" When she moved her hand, she winced, unable to hide her pain. "A friendly bet on something that I promise won't be fun for you."

Garrison leered, his gaze roaming from her face to her chest and lower. "Oh, I am a betting man. I would love to make this interesting. What are the stakes?"

For the first time all night it occurred to Lawrie that these men could do worse than physically beat her. Was it possible that her father had been completely wrong? Were the vampires he'd so thoroughly trusted really the enemy? She was beginning to believe that was the case.

"If I defeat you like I did him, you tell me everything you know about my father and you let me go." Fumbling for her weapon, she winced again when her right hand brushed over the small of her back.

She knew full well she wasn't going to get an opportunity to bring this man to his knees as she had with the last one. He was expecting it. She'd need to use a much different tactic.

"Careful, Lawrie, he's tricky," Reade said.

She glared at him. "Don't call me that."

He raised an eyebrow. “That is your name.”

Her challenger chuckled. “Crazy little firecracker.”

“Crazy?” Rage bubbled inside Lawrie. She’d been called crazy far too many times.

As if on autopilot Lawrie moved without considering what she was doing, seeing everything around her in bright, vivid detail.

She rushed forward, closing the space separating her from her opponent without either man responding to her move.

Garrison’s eyes widened. His mouth dropped open just as she reached him. They toppled to the floor, Lawrie landing on his chest. Before he could get his wits, she pulled the stake from her waistband and using both hands, aimed it at his heart and brought it down hard and fast. “I’ll give you crazy.”

The man beneath her froze. The smartass look on his face melted away, replaced by shock and then recognition.

Lawrie pressed the stake to his chest until she was certain the razor sharp tip pierced his skin. She’d grown up hearing about vampires and how her father had been a vamp-lover, how he’d betrayed his people to help save the disgusting beasts. She’d read about the vampires her father and uncle had known in her father’s notes and in the journals her uncle published for everyone at Panthera to study.

She’d seen pictures. But she’d never seen one up close. They’d been mythical creatures until tonight.

"Start talking, vamp."

"That was quite impressive, little firecracker." Garrison shifted, causing Lawrie to lose her balance, but rather than fall off or have to use her broken hand to catch herself, she bore down on the stake with her left hand, jabbing it into his chest. He hissed and his fangs descended.

A small stain of blood colored his shirt right above his heart.

"Don't try that again or I swear I'll kill you where you lie," she said.

CHAPTER FIVE

The stench of burning flesh permeated the air. Reade knew instantly the stake Lawrie pressed to Garrison's chest was no ordinary piece of wood.

"There's silver in that stake," he said.

"No shit, Einstein," Garrison snarled.

Reade didn't move. He sat stone-still watching as yet again the little psycho managed to prove a more worthy adversary than expected. He had to admit he was impressed. He also had to admit he should have stopped her from getting the upper hand, but he hadn't quite seen this coming.

He'd clearly seen her struggling to retrieve whatever was behind her back, but he'd anticipated a gun or maybe, if he stretched his imagination, a stake, though certainly not one lined with silver.

If he'd known she had a stake enhanced with silver, he still would never have anticipated her speed. She moved like a vampire. Nearly as fast and absolutely as skilled. This must have been why she'd been able to break his face, twice, when she attacked him.

That could be the only explanation for how she bested him. The question remained: how could she possibly be that fast after all this time?

"How did you do that?" Reade asked.

"Shut up," she snapped. "I'll pin his heart to the floor."

The pool of blood on Garrison's chest grew. His skin had already taken on a grayish tint. "Get her off me." His jaw clenched tight.

Reade knew Garrison was in agony. He knew all too well what silver pressed against vampire skin felt like, and he wouldn't recommend it to anyone.

"We had a deal. Tell me what you know of my father." She leaned on the stake.

"It's going to be really hard for me to tell you if you kill me," Garrison growled.

"Then tell your friend to tell me," Lawrie said.

Reade couldn't help but enjoy the moment. It wasn't just that he was intrigued by how she'd managed to make this happen or that he loved seeing Garrison's ego deflated. It was the absolute irony that made it even more fabulous.

He considered squatting down so he could see her face, but based on her ability to move much more quickly than he ever seemed to anticipate he decided to remain in his seat.

"Exactly how do you plan to end this situation?" He couldn't wait to hear what she had in store.

"I will kill him."

Garrison writhed beneath her.

"I have no doubt you will, but believe me when I say you won't kill both of us." Reade stood from the barstool and stepped behind her so she couldn't see him at all. "Tell me what your plan is to escape with your life after this."

"We had a deal."

"No. We did not. We never shook on it. And we certainly didn't agree to let you torture anyone and then leave." Reade grinned.

"You are just as my uncle said. You can't be trusted. You planned to kill me when you came in tonight, didn't you?" She turned her head an inch or two.

Garrison's hands came up, and quick as a vampire Lawrie's head jerked to face his. Her weight shifted, centering over the stake, its point cutting further into his chest. Blood bubbled from the wound.

"One more inch. Go ahead. Tempt me." Her blonde hair swung forward, covering Garrison's face.

"Reade!" he hollered and gasped, his hands returning to the floor. "Get her off!"

"What exactly has your dear Uncle Raymond said about us?" Reade sat on the edge of the booth nearest his friend and Lawrie.

"That you're ruthless blood suckers. That Father's death was your fault." She grunted. "Killing you might…"

Her voice trailed off, and Reade couldn't quite hear what she mumbled.

"Interesting. I'd say the same about him. I think most vampires who knew Raymond would agree." Reade saw the way her hand shook. Sweat now dripped down her arm. Her back was drenched. She couldn't possibly hold out much longer. Her strength had to fade soon.

"He's not a vampire, if that's what you're getting at." She pulled her legs up closer, managing to sit back and still keep the half-inch tip of the stake buried in Garrison's chest.

"Just because he doesn't drink the blood, doesn't mean he isn't a vampire of sorts." Reade sighed. "We know he's been experimenting. We just don't know what he's planning."

Of all the men Reade had met in his long life Raymond Tyrone was the most ruthless and vile. Reade had seen him slice a child's throat to ensure the family's bloodline ended.

He'd come to believe Raymond was a man from the Middle Ages reincarnated in the twentieth century. He had no doubt Raymond had spent a couple centuries in hell honing his skills before coming back to life.

"What did your father's notes say about us?"

Lawrie glared over her shoulder. "What are you talking about?" Her breaths came short, shallow and quick.

"What is it you want to know? How your father died?" Reade asked.

She nodded.

"Uncle Ray-Ray stabbed him in the back, and not just figuratively."

Reade relived that night every single time he dreamed. The horror of what had happened to a good friend was hard to forget.

"How?" She swallowed loudly. Her shoulders tensed.

"Raymond called in a report that rogue vampires had attacked Panthera and he needed help defending the lab. We arrived as quickly as possible, ready for battle." In his mind's eye Reade saw the smoky hallway, the flames from the laboratory and the screaming shadows running past him desperately searching for an escape.

"As quickly as possible? I heard it took more than an hour for the *Guards* to arrive." She ground out the words. "Turned out to be an inside job. Bunch of vamps turned on us."

"We could hardly see what was happening. Do you know how loud flames can roar?" He remembered the sound as deafening. Flames rolled over the lab, wave after wave. "Your father was in the microbiology suite, fighting with one of the attackers."

"Which of you turned on him?" Lawrie choked back tears. "Which of you monsters tricked him into trusting you and then killed him."

"An inside job is right, but not one of us, not the Guard, never one of us."

"Liar!" She sat up, raised the stake a few inches and thrust downward.

Reade grabbed the end of the stake, stopping Lawrie from driving it into Garrison's chest. "He fought hard. He fought well. He died with a stake driven into his back at the hands of your uncle."

Chapter Six

Lawrie's body shook. The combination of sheer exhaustion, excruciating pain and hearing Reade tell her something she'd long suspected was almost more than she could take.

When the vampire beneath her scrambled backward, she fell over. Agonizing pain shot up her arm, and she crumpled to the floor, screaming.

"Serves you right." Garrison crawled away, keeping his eyes trained on her. "If you weren't Lawrence's daughter, I'd rip your throat out. Where's the damn bartender? I need a drink."

His skin was gray. Veins zigzagged just beneath the surface like worms dying in the summer sun. "You were a lot nicer when you were little." He reached up for the bottle of whiskey on the bar and swallowed several mouthfuls. "Should have known Raymond would turn you into a monster."

He ripped his shirt open to reveal a festering sore on his chest. "This is fucking killing me. What's that thing laced with?" He glared at the stake Reade held with a napkin. "I felt it leaking into me every time she leaned on it."

"Has to be some sort of silver alloy. It burned my hand the second I grabbed it." Blisters bubbled over the palm of the hand he'd used to wrench the stake from Lawrie. The skin of every finger was swollen worse than Lawrie's broken fingers. "Impressive and terrifying that Raymond has managed to design something like this."

"You can say that again." Garrison climbed into another booth and closed his eyes. "That fucker has been busy. His newest weapon is some sort of evil."

Lawrie watched as the sore on Garrison's chest bubbled and oozed. She tried not to smile. Her uncle hadn't designed her weapon. He was too busy writing his books on the vile vampire subculture and overseeing the construction of his new labs to create something this potent. The pump-powered stake was all Lawrie's work.

"Feels like every drop of energy was sucked from my body." His eyes opened slowly, and all his anger seemed to focus on Lawrie. "Don't get any ideas, little firecracker." He snickered at her. "I *will* kill you next time."

Lawrie couldn't tell if he was a complete idiot or if he was playing with what she believed to be false bravado. She pushed herself up to a seated position. "Is that some sort of joke? I could have *killed* you."

"But you didn't. Trust me. You won't get another chance."

She grimaced as several more shocks of pain crashed over her.

Garrison stared past her, focusing on the door at the back of the bar. "I can't even call the bartender."

Reade walked to door. "Mic, you're needed in the bar." He returned to the booth he'd vacated, still studying the stake, testing its heaviness. "Lightweight. A pound at most."

The bartender lumbered into the bar.

"He needs a drink." Reade nodded toward his friend. The bartender walked to Garrison and knelt before him.

"He's not going to—" Lawrie gasped when Garrison lurched forward, fangs extended.

He latched onto Mic and drank, all the while keeping his eyes locked on Lawrie.

She felt his anger. It filled the room with each swallow, getting more and more intense. She was certain that when he had his strength back, she was going to wish she'd stayed at Panthera tonight.

She backed as far from him as possible, her heart thundering. There was no way she'd make it out the door and away from here before he finished. Not to mention she was fairly certain Reade wasn't letting her go either.

What had she done?

Mic's breathing slowed. His body slumped against Garrison, and the vampire easily held him in place.

"He's killing him." Lawrie couldn't believe what she'd caused. She'd provoked a vampire and now she watched him kill an innocent man. "Stop it!"

She scooted along the floor as quickly as she could and smacked the side of Garrison's head.

The vampire stopped drinking and dropped Mic onto his lap. "What the hell was that?"

Reade roared with laughter. "I'm not sure what was funnier—her bumpy dash across the floor or your face." He placed the stake on the end of the bar.

"I barely saw her move." Garrison picked up Mic and laid him on the bar. "I haven't been slapped in at least a week, and I've certainly *never* had a stake stuck into my chest." He turned to face her. "What secret do you have to share, Ms. Lawrie Firecracker Tyrone?"

Reade swooped down and pulled Lawrie to her feet. "You've had your last chance at kicking the crap out of us." His relaxed expression confused her.

He no longer seemed angry, rather he seemed amused. His dark blue eyes reminded her of Prussian Blue, one of the chemicals she'd used dozens of times in the lab. She'd always loved that color. Something about it made her feel free.

Reaching forward, he gently cradled her face in his hands. "I'm going to pat you down to make sure you don't have anything else we'd want to know about. Do you have any weapons hidden anywhere?"

She shook her head.

"You're certain?"

She nodded.

"Don't lie to us. We don't like to be lied to." Reade inhaled, and Lawrie thought his lips tugged up into a quick smile.

"I'm not." She stared into his eyes.

His gaze focused on her face and something in Lawrie's gut clenched.

She couldn't figure out what or why. She just knew that it forced her to tighten every muscle from her belly button to her toes. Clamping her mouth shut, she swallowed hard.

"You all right?" His thumbs brushed over her cheeks.

She nodded and swallowed loud enough, she was sure, to be heard in the street.

His hands slid around her neck and into her hair, fingers fanning her long blonde tresses out behind her. As each lock fell against her back she shivered.

Once he'd finished with her hair his hands returned to her neck. That's when she realized how warm they were, one more than the other, the burned and blistered one. Gently they moved down her neck to her shoulders. Her mouth was suddenly very dry. She tried to swallow and nearly choked.

"This will be over in a minute, and you'll have a drink." He moved his hands over her shoulders and down her arms, circling his palms around her biceps and trailing them down to her wrists.

When he reached her hands, he paused for a split

second, his gaze meeting hers, then traveling to her mouth. With tender, yet firm pressure his hands returned to her shoulders, gently traveling to her chest and over her breasts, slowly gliding around and under each one.

Lawrie trembled and felt her nipples respond to his touch, tightening to peaks beneath his palms. Trying not to react further, she held her breath. For God's sake, a vampire was patting her down like a common criminal in a bar with an audience, and she was feeling aroused. Not that she should feel aroused at being patted down by anyone or by having a vampire touch her, but the fact of the matter was she couldn't decide which was more exciting.

Was she crazy? She was not a criminal. And he was not a cop. But that didn't mean she didn't like playing the part of bad girl and certainly any cop who looked like this guy was bound to be a girl's dream.

But he was a vampire. One of the bad guys. One of the men who'd turned on her father and not only left him for dead but helped to orchestrate his death. She shook off the little fantasy playing in her mind and focused on the fact that this Reade was a not-to-be-trusted killer.

His hands roamed lower, sliding down her ribcage to her waist. He squatted, patting around her sneaker, then ran his hands along either side of her left leg, allowing them to glide from her ankle up her calf, gently squeezing as he went. The tips of his fingers scorched up her thigh, leaving a delicious trail from her knee straight to her crotch.

She tried desperately not to wiggle when his hand

rubbed against the juncture between her legs. Her success at not moving required focus, which meant she couldn't be in control of every other possible response.

She squeaked, a breathy squeak that only fueled her already flaming hot cheeks.

When he did the same check of her right leg she thought for sure she might orgasm where she stood.

She tried not to squirm, but she couldn't help herself. She'd never been frisked before, and this didn't quite seem like what she'd seen on TV. It felt far more intimate than watching a cop pat down a perp.

"Now for the backside." Reade spun her around.

She found herself facing Garrison, who watched from a few feet away, the most perplexed look on his face.

Reade once again ran his fingers through her hair making her scalp tingle. His hands smoothed over her neck, down her back to her hips. Simultaneously they rubbed over her ass, lingering for barely a second's hesitation.

"Well, seems like you're unarmed."

Lawrie's gaze connected with Garrison's, whose lips curled up and to the left in a lecherous grin. He had enjoyed watching his friend fondle her. That dirty little pig. She felt her cheeks burn with absolute embarrassment.

Spinning around, she raised her left hand to slap Reade, but he caught her wrist.

"Woah. What's that for?" He backed her toward a stool. "I told you what I was going to do."

"You seemed to enjoy it quite a bit!"

"What?" Reade's eyebrows pulled together. "What are you talking about?"

"I know what you were doing. He knew too. He watched and he liked it!" She pointed at Garrison "How dare you? Both of you!"

Lawrie glared at Reade. Just who did he think he was, feeling her up under the guise of patting her down? Did he think she didn't know what he was all about? She knew perfectly what he was trying to do, what he'd done.

She may not have been very experienced in life events and such, but she knew a pervert when she saw one.

Reade's head cocked to the side. "Just what do you suppose I was doing?"

"You were accosting me. I felt the way you squeezed me, my parts, my…you know what you did."

Reade looked at Garrison, who laughed.

"Oh, my, my, my. She is right, of course. I saw you squeezing and touching her parts. But you were far too quick for a regular girl to realize that you were actually copping a feel." Garrison's grin widened. "So what I want to know is how exactly *she* realized this slightly more intense, though not at all inappropriate pat down was occurring. She has a lot of explaining to do."

"I was not copping a feel." Reade stepped back from Lawrie.

"Right. Right. No, you weren't palming those lovely

breasts or giving her perfect thighs a little extra attention. Of course not." Garrison used a napkin from the table to dab at the liquid oozing from his chest where his wound, though well on its way to healing, was still visible.

Lawrie clamped her lips tight and crossed her arms over her chest, then quickly hissed from the pain of bumping her broken hand.

"She attacked both of us. I was trying to make sure she didn't have any other weapons," Reade argued.

"Of course. The groping was all in the line of duty. I've used that argument myself, several times in fact." Garrison frowned at the wound on his chest. "Though I honestly think I should have been the one to get to use it this time based on the extent of my injury. I still have this hole in my chest."

"Yeah, well you're healing. I still have a broken nose and a broken face. Not all of us have had the opportunity to feed." Reade grumbled something more under his breath, but it was spoken too low for Lawrie to understand.

Garrison laughed.

"Don't get any ideas." She leaned back from Reade, absolutely certain she did not want him to do to her what Garrison had done to Mic.

Father's notes had detailed what he believed to be the process for making a vampire. Uncle's notes had been different, similar, but with one distinct difference. According to Father the process required a blood exchange, meaning the vampire had to not only drink the blood of the victim, but he had to share his own.

In Uncle's version the exchange was optional. The vampire needed only to drain a victim dry and bury him in the soil of that vampire's roots.

Lawrie wasn't sure whose theory to believe. What she did know for sure was she had no desire to find out first hand.

"That's your own fault." Garrison's left eye narrowed, his attention on Reade. "You're the one who made the promise. Though I don't see what that has to do with sustenance. I even think Lawrence would understand."

Looking from one to the other, Lawrie tried not to panic. Garrison was convincing Reade to bite her. She wouldn't have it, at least not willingly.

"That's enough." Reade reached for the whiskey. "A man stands by his word, doesn't falter under pressure."

"Yeah, yeah and all that crap. But when the situation is dire and the need—"

"Enough." Reade sat beside Lawrie. "Tell us what your uncle has planned."

"I will not tell you a thing." She squared her shoulders and stared straight into his eyes.

Expecting to be mind-controlled like poor Mic had been, she waited, but felt nothing, not even the slightest bit odd. It made her wonder if Mic had felt Garrison persuading him to be bitten.

"Well?" she asked. How long was it going to take for

him to control her? What if they tortured her all night? What if they picked at her mind, memory by memory, until all that was left was a babbling idiot? "Just please kill me. Don't leave me here like a vegetable."

Lawrie knew if her uncle found her outside the compound and God forbid in a vegetative state he'd use her in his experiments. He'd even try to find a way to torture her in an attempt to get every bit of information out of her.

And she had secrets she didn't want to share.

"Kill you?" Reade shook his head. "Afraid not."

"At least not tonight." Garrison used a bar towel to roll the stake back and forth on the bar. "Looks deadly enough if you didn't have any idea it's part silver."

Lawrie said nothing.

Reade's eyebrow rose. "Tell us the construction of Raymond's newest weapon."

She didn't respond.

"It's not nice to keep secrets, little firecracker." Garrison smirked at Reade. "Not nice at all." He held the stake in his hand, the towel protecting his skin. His wound was healing quickly, though his skin was still gray and several veins continued to pulse. "At the very least tell us how it is you can track vampire movement."

Lawrie slid off her stool, standing away from both men. *Track vampire movement?* This must have been a side effect of the experiment, something she'd never hypothesized. How long would this ability continue? How would she measure it if she never saw another vampire? What other effects was the blood having on her?

What she wouldn't give to be in the safety of a laboratory under proper conditions.

"Better yet, tell us how it is you can move like a vampire." Reade slid the stool over to Lawrie. "Sit."

Under no circumstances would she reveal even one secret, not unless they forced it from her and even then she'd prefer to die with them all. There wasn't a soul alive she trusted enough to share her secrets, not vampire or human.

She glanced toward the back. Beyond the first door was a short hallway with a couple doors off the sides and one straight back. That back door had to be the exit.

"Don't even think about it." Garrison blocked the path leading to the door. "I'm just aching to see if you can withstand having this pierce your skin better than I did."

Reade patted the stool. "Sit. We promise not to bite you, if you promise not to do anything else that would—"

"Hurt," Garrison interrupted.

"…provoke us," Reade finished.

"Not that you have to really worry about us. Promises and such." Garrison frowned at her. "Though, I think even your father would forgive us if he saw what you've done tonight."

Lawrie sighed and plopped onto the stool. She wasn't giving up her secrets to these monsters. She knew Uncle

Raymond would just as soon kill her if he thought she'd told them anything.

Garrison held the stake between his thumb and forefinger, pointing the tip straight up. "Tell us about your uncle's latest invention." He studied the weapon, his face only an inch or two from the wood.

"Careful, would hate to see you poke your eye out." Lawrie sat back in the stool.

The pain in her hand was like nothing she'd ever felt before. It radiated up her arm, into her shoulder. Even her chest ached.

Her swollen hand looked like a puffy blue, black and red lobster claw. Her stomach turned when she looked at it.

"The tip of this stake is sharper than any I've seen." Garrison placed the stake on the bar and walked around the back. "Well, looky here." He held up a bottle of whiskey. "That old coot has been holding out." He poured three shot glasses. "Drink up, firecracker. It'll make your hand feel better."

He refilled his and Reade's glasses as soon as they'd both drunk their shots.

"Does your uncle know you have that stake?" Reade asked.

Lawrie shook her head.

"He was never the type to let valuables out of his sight. I'm surprised you were able to get your hands on it and even more surprised you were able to get out from under his thumb for an evening."

Lawrie didn't say a word. There was no need for her to speak. He hadn't asked a question. She'd learned the hard way only to speak when needed. Offering too much information always put you in a bad position and often times hurt a lot more.

"Do you think he's sent her here to spy?" Garrison asked.

"Could be, though I doubt he'd send out his most valuable possession."

"How would he have known we were in town?" Garrison knocked back two more shots of whiskey.

"Haven't you had enough?" Lawrie asked. Exactly how much could one man drink and still remain standing?

Garrison flashed another smile. "Are you monitoring how much I drink? Is it really any of your concern? After this…" He pointed to his chest. "I've earned a drink or two or twelve." Bringing the bottle of whiskey to his lips, he tilted his head back and drank until the liter was empty.

"I hope he's not driving," she said. The last thing in the world she needed to add to her list of bad things that could happen in one night was for some poor victim to be mowed down by a drunk vampire.

"Alcohol does not affect us as it does humans," Reade said. "We just like the taste. And the memories." He slid her glass closer. "You should drink. It'll numb the pain."

She wanted the pain to subside, but she also needed to keep her wits about her. Fear that she'd wake up a vampire kept her from sucking the shot down like she'd seen men do in movies.

She was amazed that with pain like this she'd been able to keep herself on track for this long.

"If you don't like the taste, Reade can always give you another dose of vampire blood." Garrison laughed. "You seemed to like it the first time."

Lawrie felt the blood drain from her face. "I…it was an acci…I was experimenting. Scientists experiment," she barked.

Both men stared at her, silent as shadows.

"Don't judge me. You have no right to judge me. I was trying to…"

They didn't move. Instead they simply watched her like she was a sideshow freak.

"We can never know for sure what's real if we don't experiment." She needed that drink. Without a second's hesitation she slugged back the shot of whiskey and slammed the glass down. Swallowing against the burn roaring down her throat, she said, "Hit me again."

Reade sat beside her unmoving. His mouth hung open. His dark blue eyes were wider than when she'd hit him.

Garrison grabbed another bottle from under the bar. "So at three years old you were conducting an experiment?"

CHAPTER SEVEN

"What are you talking about?" Reade said.

Lawrie fidgeted. "What's he talking about?"

"Did you drink vampire blood again?" Garrison refilled her glass.

"What do you mean 'again'?" She reached for the whiskey, and although her stomach turned and her skin had taken on a green tinge, she brought the drink to her lips and swallowed it back. "How did you know about the other time?"

"Well, of course we knew." Garrison poured more whiskey and nudged the glass closer.

She looked down, and Reade could imagine the thoughts flying through her mind. Her eyes flitted from left to right as though she was running through some memory, trying to understand how something happened.

He was shocked to think she could remember that day. She'd only been three at the time, and Lawrence, though he was clearly heartbroken with worry, remained calm in front of her, never once reacting like any parent whose child had just gotten into the cleaning supply closet and ingested some toxic chemical.

Reade remembered getting the call from Lawrence to come as quickly as he could. Forcing back the deluge of tears until his little girl had finally fallen asleep, the poor scientist broke down in an uncontrollable panic.

That was the night Reade promised his own life for Lawrie's.

Dropping her shoulders back, Lawrie raised her head. "Fine. I did it. What are you going to do about it? It was mine, my father's, which makes it mine. You have no rights where this is concerned."

Reade studied her face. Her eyes had been brown before she'd gotten into Lawrence's supplies. When she awoke from her nap, they were as blue as his. Their color had faded a bit over the years, but they were still blue.

No one knew what the side effects would be, or even if there were any. For several weeks they'd taken turns keeping her hidden from Raymond, who was perfectly pleased not to have to be with her, seeing as she was the only girl and thus would not carry on the Tyrone name.

Garrison cleared his throat. "Earth to Reade. Come in, Reade." He snapped his fingers in rapid succession. "You want to explain this or do you want me to take this one."

Reade shoved Garrison's hand away. "What of your father's notes? Have you found them all?"

She nodded, looking from Reade to Garrison. "I have them."

"You found the room?" he asked.

A jagged breath escaped her.

Reade waited for her answer. If she'd found the room, then she probably had more questions than she knew what to do with.

"What room?"

"She's lying," Garrison said.

"I'm not." She sat up tall, leaning forward in her seat and curling her fist. Her eyes darted to the left where the stake lay on the bar.

Garrison shifted his weight, stepping closer to the bar and squaring his shoulders.

"Really?" Reade looked from Lawrie to Garrison. "Are you two going to have another go of it now? She bested you once. You sure you want to try it again?"

"That was luck and a silver weapon. She's unarmed now." Garrison used the bar rag to push the stake out of her reach.

"She's also been drinking vampire blood, which explains why she's so damn fast."

Lawrie fidgeted in her seat. "Stop talking about me like I'm not here."

"Why did you drink the blood again? Did you like the taste?" Garrison asked. "Maybe you've got a craving for it."

A wild and savage whirlwind of emotion rolled off

Lawrie. Her body practically hummed. He couldn't tell if it was anger or fear.

"What if that's a side effect? What if once they taste it, they want us?" For a split second panic passed over his face. "What if she's an addict?"

She scowled. "I told you. I was experimenting."

"On vampires?" Garrison's voice was a deadly growl.

Lawrie sat back. "No!" She shook her head. "I've never met one before meeting you."

He curled up his lip and dropped his jaw, making a show of his fangs. "Where'd you get the blood?"

Lawrie's heart pounded faster than it should. Reade had noticed how erratically her heart beat from the moment he walked into the bar. He was sure Garrison could hear it, too.

"Do you have vampires trapped in Panthera? Where are they?" Garrison's voice sounded nearly demonic.

Lawrie's face turned bright red. Her breathing sped. Sweat dripped along her neck. Her heart was in overdrive.

When she'd been rambling on about her life, her heart beat furiously. At one point he wondered if she wasn't going to keel over with a heart attack. When she fought with them, her heart slowed to a near stop. He was confounded by what was happening but too shocked by her behavior to focus on it.

"No. No, I don't know. I've never seen any vampires in the building." She shook her head. "He wants one, but he's never caught one as far as I know."

At a volume so low Reade was sure Lawrie had to strain to hear it Garrison growled a warning. "If you're lying to us, we'll rip your heart out and eat it."

Lawrie gasped and her hand went to her chest. "I'm not," she whispered.

Reade's eyebrows pinched together. "We will not eat your heart." He glared at Garrison. "Knock it off."

Garrison backed down. "Can't trust her. She tried to put a stake through mine."

"Can't say I blame her at this point." Reade reached for Lawrie's broken hand, and she jerked away. "We're not going to hurt you." He took her hand.

He couldn't help but touch her. He'd missed her. Twenty years of searching for someone who was supposed to be dead would do that to a man. Never mind the fact that her accidental consumption of his blood when she was three had irrevocably linked them.

"I hope you know what you're doing." Garrison's attention centered on Reade and Lawrie's hands. "This could be a trap. She could have been sent here to lure us back."

Shaking her head, Lawrie said, "No. I wasn't. I swear. Raymond would…he'd never trust me with any assignment like that. He…I've never been allowed to participate in anything important."

"Just the same, if this is a trap, you won't make it out alive," Garrison said, his words a clear warning for both Lawrie and Reade.

The feel of her hand in his own stirred something deep within Reade, something familiar, yet very different. He had always cared for her as a child. It was impossible not to, but now seeing her as a woman and not a chubby little baby he felt a new longing, a need he had never expected would happen when he thought of Lawrie Tyrone.

"Lawrie, if you've been drinking vampire blood, then you found the room." Reade's thumb brushed over her knuckles. He fought the desire to give her more blood to help heal her broken hand. "I'll assume that if you're sitting here alone, then Raymond doesn't know about the room."

"No. He doesn't." She sighed.

"How much blood did you drink?"

She shifted in her seat. "Not much. One or so." Her breathing hitched and she cleared her throat.

Before the incident Lawrence's inventory of Reade's blood had been extensive. He'd taken at least a dozen pint-sized bags from Reade. Lawrie had consumed two by the time he found her.

"By one do you mean an ounce?" She had to be more wary about drinking blood now that she was an adult.

She bit her lip. "A full bag."

"A full bag!" Garrison yelled. "Have you lost your mind?"

"If I don't return to Panthera, Uncle Raymond will tear the place apart looking for me. He'll find the room. Then he'll come looking for me and he'll find you."

"Or so?" Reade asked.

"Or so? Or so what?" Garrison poured another shot of whiskey into Lawrie's glass, but before she could reach for it, he'd already emptied it into his own mouth and started pouring again. "I never should have agreed to let you come with me. You've been getting that crazy look in your eye these last few nights." He raised the bottle at Reade. "Crazy. Like an animal gets when there's a bitch in heat somewhere in the neighborhood."

"Or so," Reade repeated, watching Lawrie fidget. She scratched her head and let her hair fall over her face. "How much exactly?"

She inhaled and squirmed in the seat.

"Lawrie." Reade held her hand, giving it a gentle squeeze.

"Nothing happened when I drank the first bag." She rolled her shoulders.

Garrison's head jerked to the left. "You drank more than one bag?" His voice shot up several octaves. "Who does that? You can't drink vampire blood. It's blood. Humans don't drink blood."

"You said you knew about the first time. Why are you acting so surprised?" She pulled her hand away from Reade. "When Raymond finds the room, he will come for me."

Her defiant stare wasn't as convincing as she might have hoped. Behind her eyes there was doubt. Did she really belong at Panthera? She had to know Raymond wouldn't look for her to save her. He'd only want her because she was Lawrence's heir, and she'd be his newest test subject.

Garrison chuckled. "No worries on that front, firecracker. At least none for us." He sat back on the cooler opposite the bar. "He can't get into that room. Only two people in the world can. And you're both sitting right here."

"And neither of us is going back to Panthera." Reade watched as defiance was replaced with shock.

CHAPTER EIGHT

"I…you…I…I am most certainly going home tonight," Lawrie said.

The audacity of these two to think she would simply go with them. She had no intention of not returning to Panthera. It was her home. She belonged there. "They expect me there. They'll notice I'm missing."

Both men sat in silence. Garrison's fangy grin widened.

"They will. They'll wonder where I am," she huffed.

"I'm certain at some point your uncle will notice. I can't imagine he doesn't keep some sort of tab on you." Reade reached for her hand again. His fingers brushed along her skin.

His gentle caress made her stomach summersault. No man had ever touched her so tenderly. Actually, no man had ever touched her, at least not since her father died.

"Though, clearly, if you've managed to sneak off the compound tonight he hasn't figured out about the room because if he had, he'd be obsessed with you and you'd have never been able to leave it, let alone the compound." Reade's thumb circled over the back of her hand, and she couldn't help but watch the slow, featherlight movement.

"I…I…" Why was he so nice to her? What kind of trick was this? Was she being mesmerized? Was he trying to confuse her?

She pulled her hand away. "You shouldn't do that." She crossed her arm over her chest and tucked her hand under her arm.

"You know you can't go back to Panthera. If he figures out you've been drinking vampire blood, he'll use you in ways you've never even dreamed." Reade's eyes darkened. "I'd love nothing more than to kill that bastard, but I'm not giving him a shot at you, not this time. He's had you trapped for far too many years. Never again."

Lawrie sat back, inching away from the anger radiating off Reade. His fists clenched on the bar, and he breathed loudly, like an animal preparing to attack.

She'd never seen a man react this way. She'd certainly seen men get mad. Nearly every time she saw her uncle he was yelling about something. Her cousins behaved in much the same way. Several times their angst was directed at Lawrie for one reason or another. But never had any of them become upset about something on her behalf.

"I haven't waited this long to rescue you from the clutches of a madman just to let you walk back into his grip." The color of Reade's eyes melted to black. "I'll not lose you again. Your father will finally rest in peace."

No one ever defended her. No one. Not even the nanny who'd helped raise her and certainly not any of the employees. Her emotions tumbled, bouncing between excitement and mistrust to hopeful then annoyance.

"You have not rescued me," she said.

"You're no longer trapped in Panthera. I'm not letting you go back to being a prisoner." Reade's eyebrows pulled together. "The Guard can provide a safe haven for you."

"You did not free me from Panthera. I walked out, well, rode my bike out on my own. I did not need you to free me." She couldn't help but set him straight. No one ever let her take credit for anything good and right. "And I don't need to be made a prisoner in some other location."

Lawrie had been the scapegoat for every bad thing that happened for as long as she could remember. If she was free now, she would take credit for getting herself to freedom. Some stranger she barely knew would not take that from her.

"And I never said I didn't want to go back to Panthera. Everyone is allowed a night out. I went out and I will go back."

"You can't go back." Garrison threw his hands up into the air. "Aren't you listening? When Raymond realizes what you've done, you'll become a lab rat." His head shook, mouth hanging open like he was trying to figure out what else to say.

"Panthera is my home. The only home I've ever

known. I don't have anything else. I don't know anyone else. I don't even fully understand how life outside the compound works."

She looked from one vampire to the other. Who were they kidding? She couldn't go anywhere. She had no idea what she'd do with herself outside of Panthera.

"Panthera is not a home. It's a compound of laboratories," Reade said.

"The only place I've ever been outside of the compound is here. And this is only the third time I've come. I can't go anywhere else."

She wasn't brave enough. She knew it. She'd never leave Panthera. *Better the devil you know than the devil you don't.*

"All that I have, everything I own, everyone I know, everything that was my father's is at Panthera." Her voice dropped to a whisper. "I can't leave."

She'd always dreamt of leaving, of having a new wonderful life where people appreciated her and believed in her ideas, but when it came down to it, she wasn't willing to give up on her father's work or his memory.

She'd only just begun to understand certain theories. Throwing them away or leaving them for Raymond to find wasn't an option.

"When did you start leaving the compound?" Reade asked.

"A few weeks ago."

"When did you start drinking the blood?" He licked his lips.

Lawrie noticed the way his tongue glided across his bottom lip, leaving it moist. She'd seen handsome men at the compound, though none had truly interested her, mainly she was sure, because everyone considered her the company pariah.

But this man, vampire, person seemed interested in her. He had a connection to her. He'd been a friend of her father's. She'd read his name in her father's notes. Was it possible he truly wasn't the scourge of the world as Uncle Raymond proclaimed all vampires to be?

"A few weeks ago."

He smiled.

She wanted to believe her father, but Uncle Raymond's pronouncements countered every single thing her father had written. And Father was dead. So who should she believe?

"That sounds about right." Garrison inhaled. "She even smells like you." He poured another whiskey. "This just explains everything."

"I don't suppose you've beaten anybody up at Panthera." Reade's voice was still nasally from the broken nose she'd given him.

"Never." She shook her head and realized the side of Reade's face was swollen and black. "I…that was completely out of character. I'm sorry. I shouldn't have done that."

She didn't know what had come over her when she hit him. It was as if she'd been driven by wild desire to make him pay, some crazy sort of eye for an eye need to get even.

"You couldn't help yourself, and I deserved it." Reade touched his cheekbone and winced.

"I've always wondered if all that talk about the link was true." Garrison grinned. "Appears so. I cannot wait to tell everyone about this. Of course, I still plan to show everyone that picture. She kicked your ass." He laughed. "Let's have a look at it again." He retrieved his phone from his back pocket. "Wow. Look at that." He held it up. "Cracked the case. Must have happened when she knocked me down. You little firecracker."

"Is he drunk?" Lawrie asked.

Reade shook his head.

Garrison leaned closer on the bar. "Look at this. Look at his face." He held the phone so Lawrie could see Reade's face twisted in pain. "He's holding his balls." He slapped his hand on the bar, still laughing.

Lawrie couldn't believe she was sitting at a bar with two vampires, one of whom laughed out loud at the other's misfortune. When she thought back to her decision to go out tonight, she remembered the anticipation of doing something exciting and hoping she'd meet someone new and interesting. Yet, she never could have imagined this.

"It has been theorized that when a human drinks vampire blood, she takes on some of the emotional characteristics of the vampire donor. In fact, your father was the scientist who helped to advance this idea."

Garrison showed her another picture. "Good ol' Lawrence. Did you know before you were born we called him Lawrie?"

She stiffened. "I'm not going to want to bite a bunch of humans when the vampire I drank from is thirsty, am I?"

Reade's mouth opened, but before he could say a word, Garrison answered. "Do you feel like biting yourself right now? I'm pretty sure the vampire whose blood you drank would love to bite you." He turned the phone. "Look at this one. There you are all teary because your hand hurts while your victim lay at your knees. That's a good one."

Lawrie looked at Reade.

"Shut up, Garrison."

"Just trying to help. What about this one?"

Reade snarled at his friend, who laughed and continued scrolling through the pictures.

Lawrie's patience for both men was wearing thin. Her hand still hurt worse than anything she'd ever felt. She was getting hungry. It was later than she should have stayed out, and she was beginning to realize she was going to have a hell of a time getting her bike home with only one good hand.

Reade scooted closer.

"You were angry and ready for a fight because that's how I've felt since your father was killed. I haven't been able to let go of my desire for vengeance since your uncle told us you'd died in the fire." He took her throbbing hand in his. "I promised your father I would keep you safe, and I have failed you both. Until now."

"You promised him you'd keep me safe?" Lawrie's heart sped. All this time someone had been interested in her, in keeping her safe, and she hadn't known.

He nodded. "I swore my life to do it." Reade bowed his head. "For years I thought I was crazy. The depression and anger were overwhelming. I knew you weren't dead." With two hands he held Lawrie's. The barest of caresses tingled along her skin.

"We came to Panthera. We asked. We searched the place, top to bottom, but Raymond stayed true to his story. 'She's dead, just like her father.' He didn't even have the decency to hide the laughter in his voice."

Reade's jaw clenched, his lip curled up and he stared at the floor. "Even sealed with a blood pact I couldn't get past Raymond. I couldn't get him to relent."

Comprehension sank in, and Lawrie's mind raced through the memories of her father's notes, his labels of the samples, all from the same donor. RH+ or RH- had been marked on every bag of cryogenically frozen blood.

"What's your last name?" she asked.

"Hayes."

"Oh God." She swallowed. "You're RH."

"Right." Reade frowned.

Lawrie's cheeks flushed. "I didn't know. How could I? I didn't know you. I don't know you. I have hardly met you." She was suddenly much warmer than she'd felt all night. "I thought the blood was marked by the Rh factor." She slipped her hand from his, careful not to bang it against the bar.

Why did she feel like she'd been caught stealing something? Actually, she felt like she'd been caught gawking at the cutest boy in school, if she had gone to school with boys or with anyone for that matter.

"There were positives and negatives." She opened her mouth, then closed it, then started again. "Are you the positive or the negative? Who's the other one?"

If she really thought about it, she knew why her father hadn't named the vampire donors. Her father always protected those he thought might end up in danger. But if Reade was one of the donors, who was the other?

Lawrence Tyrone had been a very careful scientist. He'd brilliantly created systems and formulas to encrypt his notes. Lawrie spent many, many hours tirelessly working to understand what he'd done.

"I drank blood from two vampires? What was I thinking?"

"I'm both the positive and the negative." Reade poured himself another whiskey. "Lawrie, there's more."

"Oh, lots more." Garrison took her picture. "Love those rosy cheeks and wide blue eyes. Almost as blue as Reade's. Such an interesting side effect."

The camera phone clicked several more times.

"Tell her the rest." Garrison tapped the phone. "Just let me set this to video. I'm certain she'll want to study her own reaction as part of her experiment." He turned the phone to the wider angle and stepped back. "Okay. I'm ready."

Reade glared. "The blood pact I made wasn't with your father."

Lawrie's mouth dropped open. *My God, he's made a pact with Uncle Raymond. He's going to turn on me.* "I knew it. You untrustworthy, sneaky, rotten bastard!" Forgetting about the pain in her hand, she shoved Reade's chest as hard as she could, sending him sprawling backward. "Positive/negative…that's the before and after factor. Before you'd made your pact with the devil and afterward. Isn't it?"

She lunged past him to yank the stake off the bar with every intention of planting it deep into his heart.

Reade's hands shot out and caught Lawrie's shoulder, jerking her forward against his chest. She fell on top of him, crashing to the floor with him.

"It's not like that. I made the pact with you." His head hit the floor like a bowling ball. "Ow. Damn it, woman. You're going to be the death of me."

Lawrie scrambled to her knees, reaching over the bar to grab the stake. "Exactly!"

"Looking for this?" Garrison stood atop the bar, straddling the snoring bartender, phone in one hand, stake in the other, a bar towel protecting his skin.

"What did you say?" Lawrie turned back to Reade. "With me? How?"

Reade's right eyebrow arched. "After you'd gotten into your father's blood supply he begged me to make the pact."

Lawrie reeled backward, falling off Reade and slumping to the floor beside him. Her father had given her to a vampire? "How could he?"

Chapter Nine

Reade stared up at Lawrie. Once again her unexpected vampire speed had taken him by surprise. He was beginning to wonder if he was losing his own skill, or if she was simply getting faster with each passing moment.

Slowly the long fingers of her left hand moved to her neck as if she was checking for a bite mark. She glared at him. "How could you do that to me? I was a baby." Her elbow came down on his sternum.

"Ow! Fuck! That hurts!" He curled onto his side. "It wasn't like that." He would be lucky if he hadn't cracked his head wide open and punctured a lung. The woman was bound to kill him one way or another this evening.

"Your father drew the blood. I drank it from a—"

Her mouth dropped open, eyes wide as golf balls.

Garrison let out a low whistle. "Probably not a good idea to provide any details."

"Never mind. The point is your father begged me to protect you, and I promised to keep you safe forever."

Lawrie's eyes closed. She took a deep breath. "What does this blood pact mean?"

Reade grunted when he sat up. "Move back at least a foot. I can't take another assault." He probed the ribs on his right side, counting two that were definitely broken and two others that hurt like hell.

Lawrie didn't move.

He met her glare.

"Let's get everyone to their corners." Garrison moved the camera from Reade to Lawrie. "We want a clean fight." His deep voice bellowed like a boxing announcer's.

"The pact ties us together. The more often I feed from—"

She snarled.

"You asked. I'm trying to explain. It's not like I've been secretly feeding from you. I haven't tasted you in twenty years." Reade had forced himself to forget her taste seconds after he'd finished drinking.

In all his years he'd never fed from a child. Such a heinous act was unconscionable. But this had been different. There was a higher purpose, one that had been condoned or blessed even by her father, his good friend.

Lawrie huffed, and he couldn't tell if it was anger or disgust, but either one meant she might hit him again. He backed against the bar.

She was right. She had been a baby when he made the

pact. He hadn't planned to ever touch her. Of course, he had planned to be more like an uncle or older brother to her, watch her grow up, scare off boyfriends, that sort of relationship.

Lawrie's eyes darted to the right, Reade looked past her to the street. A few men walked by, mumbling. With vampire senses he easily heard their conversation, complaining about work. Seconds later they turned the corner and headed up the side street. Lawrie's attention returned to Reade.

The plan was to be there for her. Not to abandon her and leave her to fend for herself with someone who didn't care about her.

"I think the pact has strengthened because of your recent drinking of my blood," Reade said.

She heaved a deep breath, and her breasts lifted, bringing his attention from her face to her chest. His gut twisted.

She blinked a very slow blink, and her lips parted.

His cock twitched. He hadn't intended not to see her grow up and then find out she'd turned into his favorite fantasy.

Her gaze traveled down his body from his face, lingering at his chest for a moment and then traveling lower. In spite of all the pain she'd inflicted on him he wanted her.

She squeaked when she looked at his groin, and then sighed.

He cleared his throat.

"Did you have a supply of my blood hidden?" She ground out the words, though didn't pull her attention from his lap.

"No."

Her eyes were darker than when he first saw her tonight. She'd begun displaying more vampire traits with each passing minute.

Something wasn't right. He'd made one other blood pact more than a century ago, and it hadn't turned out like this. He'd never had desires like this.

Everything about this situation was entirely different.

"How much of my blood have you consumed?" Reade asked.

"Not enough for it to be lethal, apparently." She tilted her head at him. Her wild blonde hair tumbled over her shoulder and hung into her lap.

"Or to be turned vampire." Garrison watched her with feigned disinterest. "Though, she does seem to be moving in that direction."

She shot him a glare that had him backing up several feet. "Is that even a possibility?"

Her tone was angry, but her scent gave her away. Lawrie was afraid.

"No." Reade managed to get to his feet. "But clearly there are side effects. How much did you drink?" He held out his hand to help her to her feet.

"All of it."

"What?" Reade's question was in stereo with Garrison's.

"Haven't you heard of limits?" Garrison stopped filming. "Unbelievable. We need to get her back to base. Serge will know what to do with her."

"I'm not going anywhere with either of you." She ignored Reade's hand and got to her feet on her own. "I'm going back to Panthera."

"What the hell is wrong with you, firecracker?" Garrison scrolled through his phone list. "Raymond plans to kill you at some point, and he'll trap you in the bowels of the compound when he realizes you've left." He put the phone to his ear. "And you've had, let's see…ten pint-sized bags of vampire blood in the last, how long, three weeks? Of course, I'm just guessing based on memory and his mood swings over the past few weeks." He nodded toward Reade.

"I'm not leaving my father's stuff in there. It's all I have." She met Reade's gaze, staring at him with hate-filled eyes.

"You see what happens when you let *this* happen?" Garrison pointed between Reade and Lawrie. "*This* is what you get. She's moody and mean like a new vampire, and she's strong and fast like a master, and she's a little bit horny, like you. She's a complete mess."

"I'm not any of those things!" She picked up a barstool, holding it up over her head.

Reade grabbed a leg of the stool. "You're proving his point."

"I was just..." She replaced the stool on the floor and sat.

Garrison walked to the end of the bar for his conversation. "Serge, we've found Lawrie Tyrone." He glanced back over his shoulder at her. "Yeah, well, that might be a problem."

"You didn't find me," she barked.

"Why are you getting angrier?" Reade asked.

Her heart rate sped. Her breathing grew shallow.

"I don't know." She looked down. "My hand hurts." She slid off the stool and stepped away from him. "I'm confused. I...I don't know what to believe or think and I'm not sure why I feel the way I do."

"Garrison's right. It's the blood and my emotions. Could be due to the blood having been frozen or could be due to the proximity of the blood to me." A hundred other theories for why she was behaving this way ran through Reade's mind.

"Could be that she likes you, too," Garrison called out. "What?" he asked into the phone. "Oh, sorry." He turned back to Reade and Lawrie. "Never mind that last part. I wasn't supposed to say—" His mouth hung open. "Got it." He ended the call. "Serge will meet us at the back entrance of the compound where Lawrie snuck out. We're going in."

"You'll never get past the guards." She shook her head. "We're too late. We needed to get in by midnight. The third shift is much more dangerous than the evening shift." She frowned.

Reade smiled. "Good. I'm just itching to kill someone tonight."

"Me too," she mumbled, then covered her mouth. "Why did I say that?"

"Ah, well, take good notes, firecracker. This is a perfect evening for you to make your daddy proud. These are the things that happen when you drink vampire blood." He raised his shot glass. "To vampires. We wander. We fight. We fuck." He tipped the whiskey into his mouth and swallowed. "Can't wait to see that last part happen.

Lawrie's mouth dropped open.

CHAPTER TEN

"It's that first building on the right." Lawrie pointed to a building marked L3, the one she'd lived in her whole life.

"What's in that one?" Garrison pointed to the massive structure on the opposite side of the compound.

"The new lab. It's where Raymond's newest experiments take place. He spends most of his time there. Most everyone does."

The new lab, building L10, was a state-of-the art, multi-floored operation with a glass dome for a roof that housed several individual labs, an amphitheater, and, Lawrie was pretty sure, an apartment for Raymond, though since her access was limited, she couldn't say for certain.

"What the hell is he up to?" Reade asked.

Lawrie shook her head. "I don't know. He's very cryptic around me. But for sure he wants a vampire. I've heard the others talking about the…"

"The what?" Reade asked.

She looked up at Reade, then Garrison and frowned.

"Just say it. We can take it." Garrison said.

"Well, they don't really like vampires."

"Yeah, we get that." Garrison's voice sounded irritated. "As if we've done anything to them."

"The cells in the basement are supposedly lined with silver and designed to withstand any vampire's attempted escape. Shackles with silver spikes on the inside were created to hold the vampire." She frowned. "I'm fairly certain everything inside the cells is made of silver except the floor."

Garrison rubbed his chest. "Well, that does sound like a torture chamber."

The lights of an approaching truck flashed beside them and all three ducked down. The truck pulled up beside the shack, and the driver exchanged a couple words with the guard, before being allowed to enter the compound.

Lawrie was finally able to see the guard. He'd been working for Panthera for about three years and was as ruthless as they came.

The area was darker than she remembered it from a couple weeks back. Not a star lit the night sky, and the moon was hidden behind a bank of clouds.

"We'll never be able to get past him. He's very fast and deadly and mean," Lawrie whispered.

"You're all those things, too." Garrison grinned down at her. "I think you could take him."

She frowned. "I'm not mean." She'd never been mean to anyone, even her cousins.

"Shut up, Garrison," a voice came from behind them, and Lawrie spun around. "This had better not be a trap," a man wearing head-to-toe leather said in a deep, gravelly rumble.

Four vampires stepped from the wooded area, gliding up to the bushes. If Lawrie thought Reade or Garrison had been scary, they had nothing on these guys.

Not one of them was shorter than six feet. Two of them had tattoos on their necks, one was bald and the last one, dressed in leather, had a spike through his ear.

"Who let Brandt out of his cage?" Garrison asked.

The leather-clad vampire snarled.

Lawrie edged closer to Reade. "Maybe you should just let me figure out my own way in. I'll be fine. I'm sure." Her voice trembled.

"They're here to help. They won't hurt you." His arm circled her waist, and he pulled her against him. "Serge. Thanks for coming. This is Lawrie Tyrone."

The bald man held out his hand. "Ms. Tyrone, it's a pleasure to see you again."

It was like meeting a bunch of fairy-tale creatures. The men around her were like nothing she'd ever seen. They certainly weren't the geeky scientist types she was accustomed to seeing.

Serge had charisma that Lawrie had never experienced before. He was bald with defined features and dark eyes that glowed. His pearly white teeth were perfect and big. He had a smile you couldn't help but admire.

She reached out her left hand and nodded, unable to peel her eyes off his chest.

Dressed in head-to-toe black like the other men with him, he practically melted into the night. Broad shoulders. Muscular arms. Trim waist.

"What happened to your other hand?" Serge brought her left hand to his lips, placing a soft kiss on her skin.

Lawrie slowly shook her head, trying to remember what had happened. "His face." She tipped her head back against Reade's chest.

Serge smiled and nodded. "I see."

"I sent pictures," Garrison said. "You guys will love them."

Muffled chuckles behind Serge drew Lawrie's attention. Three sets of eyes glowed behind the vampire in front of her. She pulled her hand back.

"You should heal her hand before we go in," Serge said.

"That's not an option at this point in time," Reade said.

Serge looked beyond them to the guard shack. "One guard, two cameras. I think we can manage that while you care for her." Serge's attention came back to Reade and Lawrie, and she'd have sworn he was looking straight through her.

Reade shifted behind her. "She's not going to like it."

Serge turned back to Lawrie. "Does your hand hurt?"

She had to remind herself not to be rude. What did he think? She had a black and blue lobster claw as an appendage. He had to know it hurt. She nodded.

"Would you like us to fix it?"

"I, well, what does that entail?" She wasn't stupid. She wasn't about to answer yes to something that could land her with fangs of her own.

"As I understand it you've been drinking vampire blood lately."

Lawrie's cheeks heated. That feeling like she'd been caught red-handed set in again. She twisted her lips to the right and stared at Serge's chest.

"Curiosity?"

She shook her head. "I was trying to understand my father's hypotheses and really I had no one else to experiment on so I had to be the one. The idea of being able to use vam…" Her voice trailed off as she realized she was telling a group of vampires more than she probably should.

"I warned you, and now look. Roosters have come home to crow." The man with the spike in his ear stepped beside Serge. "God only knows what Raymond has done with the blood you gave him."

"I didn't give any blood to Raymond," Reade snarled, his fangs descended. "I gave it to Lawrence."

Anger vibrated in the air. "This is probably all a setup to trick us into returning to Panthera. A trap." The spikeeared man stepped closer. "Your stupid obsession is going to get us all killed."

Lawrie felt her heart slowing. Everything around her appeared in crisp detail despite the fact they stood in pitch darkness.

"You never should have made the blood pact. No good ever comes of them." The man standing before them inched closer to Reade so that they were nearly nose-to-nose. "But you already knew that."

Feral desire pulsed inside Lawrie. Her shoulders dropped back, muscles aching in her arms and chest. She wanted to rip this guy's head clean off his shoulders.

Reade twisted Lawrie to the side, moving her out from between the two men. "Remain calm, Lawrie." His arm tightened around her waist. "No need to waste your energy on Brandt."

"It wouldn't be a waste." The dark and deadly sound of her own voice surprised her.

"Interesting. Step back, Brandt. Now is not the time, and frankly I don't see how you'd be able to take both of them." Serge looked from Reade to Lawrie. "It seems they come as a pair."

Brandt snickered and stepped back. "If this goes south, I'm coming for you." He glared at Reade. "You're not getting away with this so easily."

Lawrie tried lunging for him, but barely moved against Reade's ironclad hold.

"I don't see why you would mind the fix to this." Serge

turned Lawrie's hand to see the underside. "It looks quite painful."

She sucked in a sharp breath as he tried to uncurl her fingers. "It's awful. Please don't do that." For a few seconds she'd managed to forget the crippling pain.

He released her hand. "Reade will heal your hand and you'll feel fine, better than fine. If decades-old blood can make you knowingly put yourself in the middle of two arguing vampires, fresh blood will probably make you fly."

"Fresh?" she asked.

Serge motioned to the other men. "Rafe, Gabe, take the cameras on those two buildings. Garrison, you take the guard. Brandt, manage the security desk in the shack. I'll deal with the patrol coming at us."

Without another sound the five vampires moved as silent as shadows.

Reade spun Lawrie in his arms. His blue eyes were darker than the midnight sky and glowed with a fire deep inside. "Don't think about what you're doing. Just drink."

"Wait. No. I don't think this is a good…" Her voice trailed off the second she caught a whiff of his blood.

She stared at his wrist. Dark red blood trickled from two puncture marks, slowly running the span of his wrist to drip on the ground.

"I can't." She stepped back. "I only did it as an experiment." She shook her head. "I don't know what this could do. The ramifications could be much worse."

"Worse than breaking your hand on my face?"

She glanced over his shoulder in time to see Brandt sink his fangs into the security guard's neck.

"Don't watch." Reade stepped to the side, blocking her view. "What do you think could possibly happen? You think you'll turn?"

"The thought had crossed my mind. And although I'm sure it's a life well worth living, it's not the way I'd hoped to live out mine." She'd been monitoring herself for the last three weeks, wondering if and when the transformation might take place. She'd figured it probably wouldn't, based on her father's notes about how the other specimen had…

Her mouth dropped open.

Reade raised his wrist.

She grabbed his arm, holding him at bay. "I've been studying his notes all this time only to realize I was the other specimen who drank the blood."

Reade nodded. "Yes. That's why we have the pact. It was accidental." His free hand rested on her neck, massaging her tense muscles. "If you haven't turned vampire by now, it's not going to happen. Besides, it's more complex than just taking a sip. We've been healing humans for years." He turned her around, pulling her back against his chest. "Just a couple swallows and you'll be fine. I promise."

"I don't really know you so your promise isn't worth much." Lawrie inhaled.

The scent of blood, metallic and meaty, came to her. It wasn't all that repulsive. Fresh blood smelled better than cryogenically frozen blood. She couldn't quite understand how she was able to smell Reade.

But through the blood she smelled him. Manly. Sexy. Spicy.

"You know me well enough. If you focus, you'll be able to feel my intentions. You'll know I have no plan to do anything but keep you safe." His voice dropped to a deep whisper, softly caressing her ear. "Close your eyes. Look within. Feel my blood coursing through you."

Lawrie closed her eyes and once again everything around her slowed. She'd have sworn she was having an out-of-body experience. She noted her own respirations, full, but fewer than normal. Her heart pounded a steady beat, much slower than usual.

She did not have to work at all to notice something different moving within her. It was like a foreign essence existed inside, hovering, waiting. Its warmth surprised her, filling her with calm.

Moving through her as if one with her, the essence wound its way around her heart, over the top and down the back, as if creating a protective covering. She felt completely safe, not at all worried about its intent.

Lawrie opened her eyes and looked up at Reade.

His dark eyes shined down at her. "You must know I have no plan to hurt you or to allow anyone else to hurt you either. Take what I offer. Heal yourself." The words whispered inside Lawrie, not just her ears or her mind, but in her heart she felt them.

"Your lips. They didn't move."

He barely shook his head. His wrist rose to her face. "Lawrie, take what you need. We have to go." Again the words whispered inside her, unspoken.

She brought his wrist to her lips and sucked at the bite mark.

Her tongue sizzled the second she tasted Reade's blood. Instant heat raced through her, spreading like wildfire over dry land.

The silent essence within coursed through her, moving faster than her own blood moved, touching every part of her and pooling wherever she ached.

Her hand tingled in a series of painful throbs that subsided before she could fully realize how much it hurt. The bones knit back together. The bruising faded.

Reade's fingers slid between hers, and he massaged her aching muscles, straightening and bending her crippled fingers, until finally she was able to work her hand on her own.

With her body pressed to Reade's she felt his heart beat against her, matching hers…or was hers matching his? She wasn't sure. What she did know was their hearts beat as one. His heart called to her.

Never had she felt so cared for. Never had anyone shown her such kindness. She couldn't remember a single time when she'd ever felt this loved.

Chapter Eleven

Reade's body stiffened as Lawrie's tongue worked the puncture marks at his wrist. Parts of him that shouldn't stiffen were harder than they'd been in several days. He knew he should step away from her, but the feel of her soft body pressed against his while her mouth latched onto his wrist made him stand his ground and pray she never stopped.

Reade had only ever experienced the thrill of sharing his blood with a human once before. It wasn't something most vampires did. It wasn't something he took lightly.

He couldn't help but massage her hand, to work away the pain she'd suffered all evening. He didn't want her to hurt anymore, not because of him or anyone else.

Blood sharing never seemed to end well. At least that's what his experience had taught him. Care enough for a human to share your blood, have your heart torn out when the human dies.

He would never have shared with Lawrie. His plan had never been to give away his own blood for any human to drink. Experiments, studies, theories. Those were all reasons to give away a little blood. A little. Not much. Just a few pints. And only to someone he wholeheartedly trusted.

That's what he'd done.

But then when the baby got into the mix his entire world spun as if on a blood-separating machine. Everything he'd ever believed, known or understood went right out the window.

Now, twenty years later, that baby was a full-grown woman, and their blood pact was getting stronger by the second. He'd loved her as a baby. And as sure as he stood with her tonight he knew he loved her as a woman.

He inhaled the scent of her, sweet, powdery. He'd missed that scent. He'd missed her smile, her laugh.

His lips brushed the top of her head, and she sighed, pulling her mouth away from his wrist.

When she tipped her face up to his, her half-closed eyes glowed like a vampire's in the night. She licked her lips and sighed. "That wasn't half bad." Her cheeks flushed. "Thank you."

The urge to kiss her, to hold her, to make love to her was nearly overwhelming. Reade hadn't felt this much desire ever.

"You're welcome," he whispered, realizing that if anything happened to her tonight, if she didn't leave here with him, he'd have to die. There was no way he could live without her for another second.

Reade pressed a soft kiss to her lips. Her breath caught, but her lips pressed up to his.

Someone cleared his throat. "He said heal her, not molest her," Brandt said.

"I got that on video, too," Garrison held his phone up.

Lawrie broke away from Reade, stepping out of his arms. She stared ahead.

"Put it away," Serge ordered.

"Fine." Garrison tucked the phone into his pocket.

"Lawrie, you're still in the original building?" Serge asked.

"Yes. I'm in the same room I've been in my whole life." She nodded. "No upgrades for me."

Reade wasn't surprised they'd treated her like garbage, though he was thankful they'd left her in an old building, one he was sure wouldn't have half the bells and whistles of the new facility. "This will make it a lot easier than having to break into the new building." He surveyed the area around them.

Brandt glared at Reade, then snickered. "What's happening in the other buildings?"

"Brandt." Serge's voice was a warning. Reade was more than familiar with the tone.

"I'm not going in until we know exactly why she's out. Don't tell me I'm the only one who finds it odd that Ms.

Tyrone has reappeared after all these years." Brandt looked from Gabe to Rafe and the brothers nodded.

Lawrie squared her shoulders. "Look. I don't need your help. I can go right back in there with no problem. I've lived there my whole life. It's not like I came looking for help."

"What did you come looking for?" Brandt stepped closer. "Rumor has it Raymond is looking for a vampire for his twisted experiments. Seems like an odd coincidence that you're suddenly here."

Anger rippled in the air, rolling off Brandt.

Reade wanted to kill him. "If you're so scared, why don't you just go home?" He knew getting into it with Brandt right here would only draw attention, but he wasn't tolerating the accusation.

Brandt's hands curled to fists.

"He does have a point." Serge stepped between them. "How have you ensured we aren't walking into a trap?"

Reade maintained his glare at Brandt. He hated to admit it, but he hadn't done anything to ensure she was telling the truth. He believed her because of who she was and because they had a blood pact. He would never betray her. Was he so wrong to think she wouldn't betray him either?

"We have a blood pact," he said.

"A twenty-year-old pact that isn't kept fresh is not good enough," Brandt said.

Serge nodded toward Lawrie. "You know what you must do."

Reade hissed at Brandt. He'd rather kill the bastard than do what he must. But deep down he knew Brandt was right. He knew he couldn't risk the lives of his brothers without knowing for sure.

Lawrie stepped sideways, keeping everyone, including Reade, in her sight. "What is he talking about?"

Reade caught her hand. "I won't hurt you." He rubbed his thumb over her now healed knuckles. "But you have to allow me to ask you a few questions." He tried to put it as simply as he could.

Her eyes narrowed. "Why doesn't that sound right?"

Reade rested his hands on her shoulders and gazed into her eyes, holding back from trying to influence her in any way. He wanted her to understand and agree to allow him to use his vampire persuasion to question her. He wanted to be sure she didn't feel forced by him.

"Because I need you to allow me free reign on the questioning."

Her eyebrows drew together and her jaw dropped open as though she might argue, but she closed her mouth and nodded. "Fine. I have nothing to hide." Her voice, though soft as a whisper, was confident and clear. "Go ahead."

In spite of having used his vampire ability to persuade hundreds, if not thousands of humans over the years, Reade was not prepared for this experience.

It wasn't just the deeper blue color of her eyes that amazed him or the fact they glowed as brightly as any vampires. It was that she focused so wholly on him without fear. She bravely met his gaze without flinching or trying to resist. Garrison had it right. She was a little firecracker.

He still couldn't believe the color had changed from sharing his blood, but he was more than happy for the physical sign that she was his.

He whispered, "Relax, Lawrie. Don't be afraid." Their connection was stronger than any he'd ever felt.

She nodded and slowly her eyes closed, her head drifting back.

"What is Raymond planning?" He kept his voice low and even.

"He wants to exterminate vampires. He hates you."

"Did he send you out to find one for him?"

Lawrie shook her head. "No. He doesn't know I left."

"Ask her why she left and what the hell she's up to," Brandt demanded.

Reade struggled not to break the connection he had with Lawrie in order to beat the hell out of the vampire behind him. But the last thing he wanted was for her to come back to consciousness and find him in a brawl.

"Why did you leave the compound?"

"I snuck out to see what the world is like." A tear slipped from under her lashes to roll down her cheek. "I want to find a place where I belong, where people like me."

Reade knew that if he ever had the chance to kill Raymond Tyrone, he'd enjoy every second of it.

"Are we walking into a trap?" He could hardly get the question out.

"No. Raymond spends all his time in his new lab. He doesn't pay any attention to me."

Reade glanced at Serge.

"Ask her why he's kept her if he doesn't want her," Serge said.

"Lawrie, why did Raymond keep you around after the fire?"

Several more tears slid down her cheeks. "He used me in experiments." Her voiced cracked. "Not any more, but before."

"We're done." Reade glared at Brandt. "Are you happy? If you're still concerned, get the fuck out." He turned back and wiped away the tears from her face. "Look at me, Lawrie."

When she did, her glossy eyes no longer held the ire that had filled them moments earlier. "Did I pass?"

Reade nodded. "With flying colors."

She shrugged. "Told you I had nothing to hide." She looked past him to the other vampires.

"We're happy to help you, Lawrie," Serge said.

"Thanks."

Reade wanted nothing more than to carry her away from Panthera, to bring her to his home where he'd shower her with love and gifts and any other thing she wanted so that she'd know just how valuable she was to him. Her insistence on getting her things nearly drove him to madness, but if this was what she wanted, he'd make it happen for her.

He scanned the building. The side door was some fifty yards away. "I don't notice any other cameras."

"No, there were only the two," Lawrie said. She stepped past Reade to stand beside Serge. "Once inside there's one camera at the door. It doesn't swivel and only covers the left side of the door. The door opens on the right. If the door isn't opened beyond fifteen and three-quarter inches, we should be able to sneak in fine."

Serge nodded.

Reade couldn't believe Lawrie knew the exact measurement. He smiled in spite of himself.

"At the first turn there's a camera that monitors both sides of the hallway. Every twelve seconds it turns." She pulled out a mirror. "However, if we enter when it's just turned to the southern corridor, we can get to the corner, wait for the turn and race to my door."

"You've done this before." Serge chuckled.

"Only recently. I was afraid before, but it gets pretty old being monitored."

Serge nodded. "You probably want to make note of the fact that vampire blood makes you brave." He grinned.

"Yeah. I guess it does." She smiled.

"Your father always said you were smarter than him. It was hard to believe, seeing how brilliant he'd been. But he was right." Serge rested his hand on Lawrie's shoulder. "You'd have to be to outsmart Raymond."

In the thirty years Reade had been in Serge's Guard he'd never seen him quite so elated, though he was fairly certain the fleeting smile didn't register with Lawrie, who tensed when he touched her and swallowed hard.

"How much are we taking out?" Reade asked.

"Just a few boxes, a couple bags of clothes, and my dad's old computer. It's all I have."

"Well, at least we'll be able to do this in one trip. Not like most of the women I know," Garrison said.

Serge cleared his throat, and Garrison shrugged. "It's true."

"You don't have to do this. I can just stay. Raymond will never know."

"We're getting you out of here." There was no turning back now that Reade had found her.

"If we're caught on camera, a signal will be sent to the security office. In less than two minutes this place will be swarming with guards." She looked back at Serge. "I'll feel terrible if anything happens to any of you. I don't even know you. There's no reason for you to help me."

Reade turned her to face him. "We're doing this because we want to. I want to. I want you out of here and safe. With me." He studied her face. "We're not leaving without you and all your worldly possessions. Understand?"

She nodded.

"Let's get this moving," Brandt said. "I've got plans in

two hours." He and Serge led the team across the lot to the door.

Lawrie used her key to open the door less than fifteen inches, then slid her hand mirror in to determine which way the camera faced. "We have to wait," she said.

Reade watched her lips move as she silently counted the twelve seconds. "Let's go." She moved to step through the door, but Reade pulled her back and went first.

There was no way he'd let her rush into an ambush.

They ran along the all too familiar corridor, ducked under the camera and darted down the hall at vampire speed, and Lawrie kept pace with ease. Reade knew the blood she'd recently consumed was part of the cause, but he wondered if the blood she'd had as a baby had done something to her development.

She opened her door and again Reade entered first. The room was sparse. She had a bed, a desk, a kitchenette and one door off to the bathroom.

"This is where you live?" Garrison asked.

"Yeah." She shoved the mini fridge out of the way to reveal a cracked spot in the plaster.

"This had been your father's office, not your home," Reade said.

She didn't have a window or a full sink to do dishes. She had the smallest bed he'd ever seen. How in the world she lived in this space without going out of her mind was beyond him.

All the money she was worth, all that her father had

done to build Panthera, and this was how her uncle treated her. Reade wondered if she even knew her own worth or if she believed this was all she really had.

Reade wanted to find Raymond and kill him twice.

Lawrie spun around and placed her hand on his chest. "Why are you angry?" She touched his face, brushing her fingers over his cheekbone. "You hurt. I feel it." She turned her face away, shoving her hair from her neck. "Go ahead."

Reade felt her concern for his injury and a second emotion—fear. He shook his head. "No, I'm fine."

"You lie." She blinked. "I'm just nervous about—"

Brandt leaned around Reade. "If you don't get on it, you may not have to worry about Reade's aches and pains." He waved her toward the secret entry. "If you make it out of here alive, there will be plenty of time for you to get used to the idea of him feeding from you."

"Open the door, Lawrie. Let's get your stuff and get going," Reade said.

Brandt was right, though Reade couldn't help but hate that they had to rush. He wanted to get her out of this place, but he also wanted every moment she touched him to last forever.

Reade reached past her and placed his hand over the crack in the plaster. The wall slid to the side, and Reade's mouth dropped open. She really had been experimenting.

Chapter Twelve

Lawrie's head spun. Her heart raced. Her stomach twisted and flipped. She'd never felt anything like what she was currently experiencing. Her own emotions were jumbled and excited, but on top of those she had Reade's emotions to contend with.

The most thrilling ache pounded in her heart. Every time she looked at Reade she felt like her heart would explode. Could she love this stranger? Did he care for her, too?

Mad excitement that she was leaving Panthera and might have a life outside the compound nearly consumed her.

But most concerning of all was the absolute terror that everything that was happening, all these wonderful possibilities, would be ripped from her and she'd wake up to find herself living her same old life of lonely despair. What if none of this was real?

Knowing she needed to keep her wits about her and not get caught up in Reade's feelings of wonderment and desire and anger, Lawrie rushed through the door. She needed to get her things and get out.

"It won't take but a minute." Grabbing her bag, she pulled the plug out of the wall for the computer and handed it to Brandt, then opened a drawer to retrieve her files, all six of them. She'd tried very hard not to write too many things down in case her secret room was discovered.

She grabbed the picture of her with her father, adding it to the bin she pulled from beneath the desk. It held all her most valuable items. "That's it."

Garrison grabbed the bin and exited the lab.

Reade stared at the containers that had held his blood. "Ten. You drank all ten." His disbelief washed over Lawrie. "You weren't repulsed?"

"No, and it was twelve, remember?" She turned him around and pushed him out of the lab. There was no sense in dawdling and now was not the time to discuss exactly how she'd felt about the experiment. At some point she probably should tell him, she should sit and thoroughly study her notes, jot down everything she remembered about the episode and tonight and anything that might happen after they leave here, but they needed to move.

Taking one last look at the twelve-foot space, she felt a flicker of melancholy. This was the last place she'd seen her father alive. She'd spent her entire life here. The fact that she was leaving it behind was almost incomprehensible.

But now she had someone who was interested in her and not just so he could kick her around.

"What do we take from this area?" Serge asked.

Lawrie pulled two trash bags from a cabinet, went to the dresser and dumped four drawers into them. "This." She held the two bags up. "That's all."

"I love a woman who travels light," Rafe said, slinging one bag over his back and handing the other to Gabe.

"Let's get the hell out of here." Reade pulled Lawrie close to him.

She sensed a surge of something, annoyance, she thought, but as quick as she felt it, it vanished.

They didn't bother to wait for the camera to turn. Instead the moment they opened the door they ran down the hallway, banged a hard left and raced for the door.

Lawrie's heart thundered. Panic filled her. She couldn't believe she was actually leaving Panthera. She was seconds from freedom. Seconds from leaving behind the only life she'd ever known. Seconds from not having to worry about being called names that were meant to hurt her.

The alarm sounded, horns blaring. The camera in the corner stayed locked on the group running down the corridor.

"Oh no." Lawrie's breath caught in her throat. Her body tensed and she stumbled. "We're not gonna make it."

Reade caught her before she fell, pulling her against his

chest and picking her up. "We're going to make it. Stop worrying."

Like a battering ram the first vampire smashed into the door, breaking through it as if he was a football player tearing through a game day banner. Everyone else followed, streaking across the lot back to the exit of the compound.

Lights from the security trucks chased them. The rapid cracking of shots sounded and bullets whizzed by their heads.

"Damn it!" Garrison snarled. He adjusted the bin from one arm to the other, taking a quick look at his shoulder. "Grazed me." He growled. "Are those silver bullets? This is not my night."

The gates to the compound clamored shut.

"Oh God." Lawrie clung to Reade. This was it. They were doomed. She was certain her uncle would make her pay with her life, and God only knew what he'd do to everyone else. "I'm sorry."

"Stop worrying," Reade repeated and launched himself upward.

The cool night air whooshed by, and Lawrie gasped at the ground pulling away as they catapulted up and over the fifteen-foot fence. Without hesitation everyone else did the same.

The group landed several feet from the gate and moved through the trees, dodging bullets and ducking under tree limbs.

"Almost there," Serge called from a few feet ahead.

They arrived back at the place they'd left Reade and Garrison's cars. Parked on either side of them were three other vehicles, two of which were motorcycles.

The tiny trunk of Reade's car opened and a few of Lawrie's possessions were loaded.

Garrison laughed. "I told you someday you'd need a bigger car." He popped the trunk of his Lexus where her slightly disassembled bike was stored, and the rest of her things were loaded. "Meet you back at your place."

"Have you already discussed next steps?" Serge stood beside the front wheel of Reade's car.

"No, but I have a plan." With swift movements Reade opened the passenger side door and placed Lawrie inside. In spite of the speed with which he moved, Lawrie registered the entire gesture and mustered the wherewithal to kick her foot out to block the door from being shut.

"Where are we going?" She may have been free from her uncle, though now on the run, but she wasn't willing to go from being Raymond's hostage to being anyone else's.

Reade's hand rested on the door. His dark eyes met hers. "For the night I'll take you to my house, where you'll be safe. Tomorrow we'll figure out where to set you up." His voice, though controlled, held an edge.

Lawrie was unsure of what the tone meant. Was he angry with her? Was he still hyped from the escape? Did he not want to be burdened with her? She wouldn't stay somewhere she wasn't truly welcome. Even if she had to borrow some money to get herself set up, she'd leave and figure a way to pay him back.

"Fine." She stared out the front window, confused. She'd thought he cared for her. She'd have bet her life that was what she'd felt from him. But now that they were free from the compound, now that she really had survived an escape, he didn't seem happy.

Lawrie wouldn't be anyone's burden. She would not let one more man make her feel like she was not worthy of existing. She'd get through this night and tomorrow she'd leave Reade, too.

"You're sure?" Serge asked.

Reade nodded and closed the car door.

Lawrie heard their muffled voices, but she didn't bother to focus on what they were saying. She didn't need to hear the words to know Reade wasn't happy. The tone of his voice said it all.

The car sped down the road. Reade drove like a madman. Of course, Lawrie had never been in a vehicle that drove more than fifteen miles per hour. That was the speed limit on the compound.

She glanced at the dials on the dashboard. "Seventy-five! Why are you driving so fast?" She gripped the door handle and pressed her feet to the floorboard, stiffening her body to a plank.

The car slowed a bit. "The speed limit is sixty-five. I'm not going *that* fast."

"Are you in that much of a hurry to get rid of me? Just pull over. I'll get my own way." Her chest hurt. She wasn't sure if she was having heart failure from the terror of driving so fast or because she wanted to cry for being rejected yet again.

Sadness swamped her. How could her life be so damn lonely and miserable? How long would she have to wait for someone to care about her enough to want to spend time with her?

She bit her lip to keep from crying. There was no way she'd let him see her sad. She'd learned long ago not to show anyone her emotions. It made too many people laugh.

Reade's hand covered hers. "I never said I wanted to get rid of you." His deep voice, though still somewhat nasally, was soft. "I never want to lose you again." He laced his fingers with hers and brought her hand to his lips.

Lawrie looked at him. The blue of his eyes shown against the lights of the oncoming cars. He kissed her hand, then glanced back toward the road.

At the next exit he pulled off the highway and into an empty lot, parking the car under a light. "I have waited twenty long years to find you."

Reade turned sideways. "In my mind I remembered you as a child, the little girl with unruly curls and a laugh that made everyone smile." He tucked a lock of her hair behind her ear.

Lawrie felt a sense of excitement rising from Reade. Her stomach fluttered.

"Maybe it's because you consumed what I'd given your father to use for his experiments all those long years ago. Maybe it's that you recently drank the rest of what was there. I don't know, but I can't stand the idea of you not being with me."

He stared straight into Lawrie's eyes and for the first time in her life she thought she might understand what it was like to be wanted. The way he leaned closer to her, the way he softly touched her cheek and let his fingers linger against her skin—it made her believe him, believe in him.

"I would never force you to stay with me or to do anything more than you want, but I can't let you go off without knowing I've done everything in my power to ensure your safety."

Lawrie reached up to capture his hand. "I know. I feel what you're telling me as if your emotions are being transmitted to me. That sounds weird."

Reade smiled. "I understand. I feel yours, too."

"You don't need to do any more than you've already done. Well, maybe you could help get me set up, teach me to drive or at least explain how to use the transit system." She shrugged.

"I'll teach you that and more." He chuckled and slipped his fingers between hers, locking their hands together. "You're no burden. Never."

Lawrie swallowed. There was something she needed to

say, something she should have admitted from the beginning, but the entire evening had gotten out of hand before she could reel it in, and they hadn't had a moment alone until now.

"Reade, I've wanted to drink those samples for a while." She couldn't look in his eyes. Somehow admitting that she'd wanted to consume vampire blood embarrassed her. Maybe it was all the years of hearing how stupid she was or how vile and disgusting the vampires were. Whatever it was, she felt ashamed of herself.

"I only discovered the room about three years ago. Once inside it took me well over a year to find the safe and several more months to figure out the code to open it. That's where I found the blood."

Her father had been a genius, and he would always be one in her mind. His system for encrypting information was second to none. But she had beaten his system, and she had found the blood.

"Funny thing was that even before I knew the safe existed the area where he'd hidden it was a place I found myself constantly. I stood in that exact spot, more times than I could count, finding myself drawn to it as if by some hidden force." She frowned. Had Reade's remaining blood been calling to what was left inside her all that time?

"I held out for as long as I could, reminding myself how dangerous drinking it would be, but finally I gave in. Who else could possibly drink it? How else would I know?" She looked into Reade's face.

His expression was neutral. "I gave it to your father for experimenting. It was fine for you to continue his work. I'm sure his plan had been to try it on himself." He paused for a moment as if remembering something from long ago. "It wouldn't have been the first time he'd done such a thing."

Lawrie nodded. She'd read her father's notes and knew about his desire to understand the impact of vampire blood on the human body as well as his fear that something negative would happen to whomever volunteered.

Reade was right. Her father had planned to experiment on himself. But he'd waited, not wanting to leave Lawrie an orphan.

She pulled her hand from his and let out a long sigh. "Reade, it wasn't that I wanted to complete my father's work." She knew she should tell him. She had to admit why she'd done it. Maybe he'd be able to help her overcome her problem.

She'd been confused and frightened by her impulses. She didn't understand them and knew that if Uncle Raymond found out about them, her life would have been a thousand times worse.

Tears welled in her eyes. What was wrong with her? "I wanted to drink it because I wanted it. I wanted to taste it and have it all for myself." She watched tears drop into her lap, unable to raise her face. She couldn't bear him looking at her. "I lied earlier. I didn't drink it over the course of a few weeks. I drank it all in minutes, like some addict trying to get a fix. It was awful and I'm ashamed of myself for doing it. What is wrong with me?"

Reade's fingers curved under her chin, and he tilted her face toward his.

She blinked a few more tears. "And now, here you are and things are different. I want you. I don't…I'm confused. I don't know if I want you or if your blood inside me wants you."

She'd never felt anything like this. Her heart ached. She had the strangest urge to kiss him and touch him. She wanted desperately to climb into his lap to be as close to him as possible.

"I am drawn to you as you are to me."

"You don't understand. I don't even understand. I don't know how or why, but I think I love you." This whole evening had been a whirlwind of emotions and strange behavior. "I've never loved anyone. I don't know if this is love or an outcome of my experiment."

She knew she shouldn't make statements that she couldn't prove and certainly didn't understand. But, what difference did it make at this point? She'd just admitted she liked drinking vampire blood. He couldn't possibly think she was any stranger.

Reade looked down at their hands, and Lawrie could feel him hesitating.

"What? What is it?" She pulled her hands away, crossing them over her chest and huffing. "Just say it."

When Reade looked back at her, she felt all his attention, every cell in his body, focused on her. "I was drawn to you before I drank what your father gave me." He licked his lips. "From the moment I met you I wanted you."

Lawrie's mouth dropped open. "I…I was just an infant when we met." Her breaths came in quick gasps and her heart picked up speed. What was he saying? What had he done?

Reade nodded. "I know."

Chapter Thirteen

Reade's own heart raced as he tried to explain. For all these years he'd thought he was disappointed, even disgusted with himself at breaking a pact, one he'd sealed in blood with her long before she could ever understand its meaning. He'd believed himself a useless failure, deserved of a long life of misery where every night was plagued by the constant nagging reminder of how he'd betrayed Lawrence and his baby daughter.

Not until this evening did he realize he was heartbroken. He'd loved her from the moment she was born. Only now did he realize what that meant.

"How could you?" Lawrie asked. Again her hands went to her neck, a defensive posture Reade recognized well.

"I didn't. I wouldn't. I could never act on the urge. Never." He shook his head. "But there was something about you that called to me, and I wanted nothing more than to be in your presence, to watch you play and hold you when you slept." Reade shook his head. "I thought it was some weird regret of not having fathered any children, some horrible joke of fate that now as a vampire the urge to parent would overcome me. And I kept on thinking that all these years."

A wave of relief rolled through the car, and he couldn't tell if it was his own confession or Lawrie's understanding that made them both relax.

"It is entirely possible that we were meant to be together." Reade watched the way her mouth opened as if to argue, but closed instead. "Drawn to one another like two parts to one whole."

He knew he sounded ridiculous. Hearing the words come out of his own mouth made him cringe. What if she didn't think that way? After all she had been only a baby. Maybe her compulsion to drink his blood came from some bizarre addiction she'd developed as a child.

A goofy grin spread over Lawrie's face. "Like soul mates? That sounds so silly." She laughed, then snorted. "Sorry. That just sounds insane, like some sort of fairy tale."

He laughed, hoping his disappointment wouldn't show. "Yeah, you're right."

At the very least she wasn't trying to beat the crap out of him, so for the moment he had that going for him.

"Fairy tales." She sighed and looked out the window into the darkness.

Reade watched her reflection. Her smile faded and

tears pooled in her blue eyes. A sadness he'd felt more times than he cared to remember descended in the car, and he realized that all this time he'd been linked to her, attuned to her emotions just as much as his own.

"Hey." He reached across her to pull her into his arms. "Don't cry. If this isn't something—"

"You don't understand. I don't know anything about romance or love or relationships. Nothing." She pushed out of his embrace. "Well, nothing good. I don't have the slightest idea what to do. I…I want this to work, to be real, but I just…"

"I hope you're serious." Reade leaned forward. "Or I'm probably about to get killed." He couldn't stop the urge to kiss her.

There was nothing more in the world he wanted than to make her pain stop. He wanted her to laugh and be happy. She deserved to know what being loved truly meant.

When Reade kissed Lawrie he nearly lost control. He'd been dying to kiss her for hours, and between the thrill of finally kissing her and the fear she might deck him, he was lost to her instantly.

Her lips were soft beneath his. She opened her mouth and kissed him with such passion he nearly climbed into her seat to take her in the car.

Desire burned through him like he'd never felt before, not with any woman, not once. He wanted her, wanted to make love to her, wanted to taste her, wanted to claim her for his own for all the world to know.

The soft moan that escaped her when she pulled back for a breath made his cock throb.

He shifted in his seat, preparing to sit back, but she yanked him to her. "Kiss me again," she said and pressed her mouth to his.

He braced himself against the car door to keep from crushing her. She was once again using her borrowed vampire speed to throw him completely off-kilter.

"Take me, Reade." The breathy command she whispered in his ear sent rapturous tingles through him. "I want you to have me."

"Not here," he managed to say, though it pained him not to do as she commanded.

In the front seat of his Corvette was not the place he wanted this to happen. He wanted her to have a more romantic, comfortable, intimate experience, and besides, there was not nearly enough room for him to do all the things he planned to do.

"We'll go home." He tried to pull back.

"No." She looked in his eyes. "I feel your hunger. You need me." Her eyes blazed, and Reade could feel her looking into his soul. She tilted her head to the side. "Take me."

Reade pulled back. "You're sure?"

"Never more." She pulled his head to her neck. "Make me yours."

Reade couldn't bother to think twice about the offer. He could barely believe what was happening. His fangs descended and he buried them into the soft flesh of Lawrie's neck.

She tasted just as sweet and perfect as he remembered, only this time he didn't beat himself up for enjoying her. He didn't tell himself what a sick and demented creature he'd become.

This time he savored what she willingly gave him, enjoying every bit of her essence.

He pulled back from her neck to see her eyes flutter open.

"That didn't hurt," she said.

He smiled. "It wasn't meant to." He cupped her cheek and placed a soft kiss on her lips. "I'll never hurt you."

"Promise." She pressed her forehead to his.

"I swear my life to it."

Thank you for reading *Her Vampire's Promise, Novella One in The Romance in Central City Series.* I hope you enjoyed it. If you did, help other people find my book by writing a review.

Excerpt from

THE VAMPIRE'S PARTNER

ROMANCE IN CENTRAL CITY NOVELLA TWO

Bright headlights lit the window seat of Central City Coffee. Alice squinted. "What the hell with the high beams? Jeez." She glared at the passing car, grumbling about idiots and morons being allowed to drive.

Hunter didn't mind the lights of the passing cars so much, and not just because they were to his back, but more because her front was fully illuminated.

He reached for the half-filled jar of coffee beans, turning it around in his hand and listening to the beans rattle. Dark roasted Sumatra beans had nothing on the color of Alice's eyes.

Hers were the darkest brown he'd ever seen, and over his many years he'd seen a lot of eyes. Mostly they'd been glazed over by the time he was done staring into them. But not Alice's.

"This was a stupid seat." She picked up her to-go cup and sipped her Earl Grey tea, replacing it in the center of her perfectly folded napkin. "I knew better than to let you pick. This is not incognito."

He barely nodded. "By incognito you mean hiding in

the back corner where no one would ever think to look for us." He gave her a full nod. "I thought I explained that being obvious is sometimes the best hiding place."

"I thought I explained that Central City is not the type of place to use your sophisticated theories." She used air quotes for *sophisticated*. "The people of this town are a lot more basic than that."

The bells on the door jingled as another customer entered the shop. The scent of freshly ground coffee beans swirled in the air.

"Which is why being right under their noses will work." He replaced the jar of beans at the end of the table. "I know I'm the senior member of our team, but do I have to teach you everything?"

"Smart-ass."

Alice turned her head, watching the activity at the counter. Her black wavy hair caught the light of another passing vehicle, and Hunter saw one gray strand streaking through her bob.

It didn't curl under her chin like all the others. Instead, it stuck straight out as if it was screaming to be noticed.

He bit back a laugh. She'd been making him pull unruly gray hairs for the last two months. Twenty-three and going gray, she'd squawked. Apparently his partner came from a long line of early grayers, as she called them. Why she worried about the occasional strand was beyond him, but then most things women did made no sense.

The lady at the counter ordered a coffee and a dozen donuts, then sat at a table in the back corner.

Alice watched the counter where another customer placed an order.

He loved the face she made when he annoyed her. Perfect eyebrows drew down. Her lashes twitched, and her lips pulled tight over her teeth. It all served to make those dark brown eyes sparkle with ire.

"Stop it." She looked out the window. "I can feel you trying to get in my head."

"Come on." He reached across the table, taking her hand in his. "We're supposed to be lovers."

When he walked into work tonight, he learned the rumors were true. Panthera Corporation was up and running again, and Raymond Tyrone was still at the helm, which meant only one thing. That evil prick was up to no good.

Alice tsked. "We're supposed to be working, pretending to be lovers, not real lovers."

Since it was a pretty fair bet that no one in Central City knew him it made the most sense for Hunter to help stake out the area. He'd been assigned to take Alice and to fit in.

"Semantics. Either way people are supposed to believe we're lovers."

"And they will. They'll think we're having a spat." She rolled her eyes.

He leaned forward. "That means makeup sex."

Just the thought of it made his gut tighten—his gut, his chest and another muscle, quite useful to lovers. He smiled. "Look at me, baby. Don't make me beg."

"Shut up, Hunter." She pulled her hand from his. "If you weren't always trying to whammy me, we wouldn't always have to pretend to be *sparring* lovers."

The word *lovers* rolled off her tongue, and his fangs ached. His tongue pressed to the back of his teeth, trying like all hell to keep them from dropping. Not an easy task when the object of your every desire sat three feet from you, unknowingly teasing you into a frenzy.

"Are you saying that if I stop doing that…" He lowered his voice to a deep whisper, one he knew worked quite well with other women. "…we could be more intimate?"

Just the thought of it made his cock rub against his zipper. It was these moments when he wished he wore underwear.

She whipped back to face him, her lip curled up and those dark eyes narrowed to a venomous glare.

Hunter could hardly keep from clearing the table and taking her on top of it. Her wild anger did things to him he couldn't quite explain. He reminded himself that getting arrested for public fornication definitely did not fall under the definition of incognito.

He smiled. "Is that a no?"

"A big fat no." She shifted in her seat, folding her arms over her chest, which he was fairly certain was a very comfortable stance for her, considering how often she used it. Guarded, yet aggressive.

He quite liked it, too. He loved the aggressive part, but the fact that it pushed her breasts up and at him made it all that much more enticing.

He reached down to make an adjustment.

"You know I love you, baby," he said in the same deep whisper, wagging his eyebrows at her.

She squeezed her red lips tight between her teeth, but the smile she was battling won out, and she grinned. "You're an idiot."

"Yeah," he said, making sure to use his sexiest voice. "Say it again. You know just what I like to hear." He sat back, his legs extended out under the table on either side of hers. "Let me try one more time."

"Nope." She shook her head, and her gaze dropped from his face to his chest, a move she'd been using for months.

He'd debated writing something on his chest like *look up* or *kiss here* or something to make her realize he knew exactly what she was doing. But the idea of her looking somewhere else because she'd been caught stopped him.

"It's for your own good. If your ability not to succumb to a vampire's gaze wanes or fails entirely, you're screwed. It's best if we know when it might be happening."

That was the absolute truth, without an iota of doubt. The fact that he enjoyed trying to mesmerize her more than he enjoyed most other things was also true, but she didn't need to know that part.

She frowned. "A preventative measure?"

"Exactly."

For as long as Hunter could remember, which was about ninety-eight years, seeing as he couldn't seem to remember anything before his teens, he always planned and prepared for the what-if scenario.

What if robbers ransacked his home? What if he found himself with no money, no food, no shelter? What if he lost everyone who meant anything to him?

He'd learned the hard way to always prepare, and he always made sure everyone he respected did the same.

"You never know when your luck could run out. You don't want to find yourself at the whim of someone far more criminal than me."

Alice had proven to be not only mentally stronger than most humans with her ability to not be influenced by a vampire, but she was also in superb physical condition, managing to hold her own in most fights with any human. That didn't mean she was safe when it came to vampires.

"Doubt that could happen." She watched a couple walk past the storefront window.

"People need to learn to be responsible for themselves and not expect someone else to take care of them."

"Did you hear what you just said to *me*?" Her tone was less than approving. "As I've demonstrated several times, I don't expect anyone to take care of me." She leaned forward and stared straight into his eyes. "Least of all some vampire."

Excerpt from

A VAMPIRE'S PASSION

ROMANCE IN CENTRAL CITY NOVELLA THREE

From the corner of Brandt's eye he saw a cell phone pointed at him.

"Don't."

"He speaks. Finally." Garrison tapped the phone. "Could you repeat that? I'd like to get it on video to prove to everyone what a conversationalist you really are."

"Your childish fetish for picture taking will blow our cover."

Without looking at him Brandt felt Garrison roll his eyes. The vampires stood in the shadows watching workers from Menhaden's, Central City's classiest restaurant and bar, step out into the warm night air. Brandt had been standing in this same spot in the hot, stinking alley for five hours. The moment the sun set he'd left the base to take his post for the night.

"Why did you come?" He hated working with a partner, hated dealing with a sidekick.

"We were assigned to this task together. We are on

high alert. Remember?" Garrison scrolled through images on his phone. "Unless, of course, you have a death wish. Maybe agreeing to follow a partner protocol was just a show and not a truthful oath."

Brandt let out a breath in an attempt to keep from responding to the man he believed to be the world's most irritating vampire. He didn't have a death wish of his own, but he'd gladly grant someone else's.

"I, of course, do not want to die or be captured and tortured by Raymond Tyrone, so it would be quite helpful if you followed safety precautions."

Brandt gritted his teeth. There was no telling what he'd missed in the few hours of daylight that coincided with the restaurant's hours of operation. It seemed unlikely that their suspect would have done his business during those hours, but he couldn't know for sure.

"Why aren't you home with your new doggie?" Annoyance laced Brandt's words.

"Dottie is home resting. You should have come to the adoption night. You might have done something crazy, like found a friend." Garrison thumbed through the pictures on his phone. "You want to see her? She's so cute curled up on my bed."

"She's probably the only female to ever do that."

"You're a real dick." Garrison snickered.

Brandt had managed to avoid the entire ridiculous fiasco of the dog adoption event, figuring everyone else would stay late and be busy all night. It gave him the perfect opportunity to do a complete surveillance alone. Apparently, his luck on the issue had run out.

"You should lighten up. You might learn to enjoy life a bit." Garrison slid back into the shadow beside him.

"I enjoy life just fine." Brandt reached up and twisted the spike in his earlobe, rolling it back and forth. As soon as the friction of the metal against his skin caused his earlobe to heat, he stopped.

"Ah, yes. You're a regular party animal." Garrison leaned back against the wall. "In fact everyone always says be sure to invite Brandt. He's the life of every party."

Brandt tore his attention from the doorway across the street to glare at Garrison.

"Hey. Don't get upset with me. If you want, I'll put out the word that you no longer want to be relied upon to entertain people, that you just want to be left alone to wallow in your own miserable existence." He shrugged. "I am here to help you, buddy."

"Don't call me buddy."

Garrison stared at a video on his phone. "Right. You're no one's buddy."

Brandt leveled one more glare at the annoying vampire. "Why the hell did Serge send *you* anyway?"

"*We* were supposed to come together, if you recall the strategy meeting. No one in the field alone until we know exactly what's going on at Panthera." Garrison's eyebrow inched upward. "Odd how that's the order you chose to ignore. Must have some sort of death wish."

The door across the street opened and closed and several suits walked out, laughing and patting each other on the back. "Very soon, Mr. Tyrone. You will have your subject very soon," a man with slicked-back hair and a shark's smile said.

"Is that Rollins with Tyrone?" Garrison whispered.

The man met the description they'd managed to reap from the memory of one of their captives, right down to his beady eyes.

"You get me what I want, and you'll be a very rich man." Raymond Tyrone surveyed the street, his steely gray eyes scanning back and forth as a long black limousine pulled up to the curb. "Very rich indeed."

"You'll get your prize. Don't you worry," Rollins said.

"Prizes." A wicked smile curved Tyrone's lips. "Let's not forget my army."

Rollins inclined his head. "Yes, your experiment wouldn't be complete without a legion to serve."

Tyrone's mouth opened an inch, but he paused for a moment. "Yes, my own military." He rested a hand on the limousine then turned to Rollins. "Say, that waitress was feisty."

Rollins smiled. "Just the way you like them."

"Get her to come willingly. Maybe offer her a little cash. They all have a price." The elusive cofounder of Panthera Laboratories slipped into the car, followed by Rollins and two other men, and the vehicle pulled away.

Brandt moved to follow.

"Ah, no chasing cars. We're to question the staff, see what they might know." Garrison kicked a pebble. "No running off on your own. Orders were pretty specific, probably for your benefit."

"I work alone."

"Not anymore. Unless, of course, your goal is to be captured and tortured, killed even, though maybe not. Maybe Raymond Tyrone will keep you alive, make you a partner in whatever he's up to. Call you his best friend. You're about as friendly as that twisted fuck."

Brandt darted across the alley, closing the ten-foot distance between them, and pinned Garrison to a brick wall by his neck. "As I said, I am no one's friend. Least of all that bastard's." His fingers tightened around Garrison's throat.

Excerpt from

HIS VAMPIRE PAST

ROMANCE IN CENTRAL CITY NOVELLA FOUR

Across the street from the convenience mart Serge studied the gas station attendant. Just as he'd done every night for more than three weeks, he stood in the shadow of the trees, watching.

Always the same routine. The tall redhead counted her drawer, made the cash drop into the safe beneath the counter, and put on her backpack. Then, from behind her bulletproof window she looked all around the gas station, squinting her lovely hazel eyes at the darkness as though if she concentrated hard enough she'd be able to see anyone lurking beyond the light.

If hundreds of years of living in the shadows hadn't trained Serge to be meticulous about keeping his presence hidden, the recent goings on at Panthera Laboratories had driven the point home. Raymond Tyrone, the surviving founder of Panthera was on the warpath with the intent of dominating Central City, and Serge was fairly certain his sights far exceeded the city limits.

Like some Pavlovian response to the thought of

Raymond Tyrone, the muscles in the back of Serge's neck tightened, sending a sharp ache up into his head and down to his shoulder blades. He rubbed a hand over his freshly shaven scalp and down to his neck, hoping to squeeze the pain away.

Since the fire at the lab twenty years ago, The Vampire Guard had been barred from Panthera, refused access as though they were the enemy. When the reality was Serge had been a silent partner in the business. A longtime friend of Raymond's late brother, he'd agreed to help finance their cancer research. He'd had no idea what Raymond was doing in the background.

A car turned onto Edgeton Road and drove up to the gas station, signaling its impending turn, but before it could pull into the lot, the lights in the store and above the pumps turned off.

Serge watched the attendant. She ducked down, peeking above the counter only high enough for the top of her head and her eyes to appear. The car pulled away, and she stood up, watching it turn off the street before she flipped the lights back on. Her lips moved, but Serge couldn't tell what she was saying, though he was certain she was speaking some irritated complaint to herself.

As always her chest rose and fell in rapid breaths as she contemplated leaving. Focusing on her neck, he watched the veins beneath her delicate skin pulse with the quickening beats of her heart. Her rising body temperature would cause her scent to perfume the little room, making her the preverbal vampire bait. Anticipation gripped him, and his fangs ached.

Never taking her attention away from the line separating the lighted area from the unknown, she moved to the door and prepared to leave the safety of the enclosed cashier's booth.

Leaning back against a tree only a few feet into the blackness, Serge waited. There was no way she could see him. Besides, he'd been working his magic to ensure she wouldn't remember him.

A twinge of disappointment burrowed into his chest. He'd done such a good job, been so careful that even when he stood directly in front of the booth, passing his money through the metal drawer for some purchase, she appeared oblivious to his existence. It was the right thing to do. Safe. But that didn't mean he wouldn't have preferred she knew him.

The memory of her sweet scent and the way she felt in his arms caused his chest to burn. He reminded himself he'd come only for nourishment, nothing more, never anything more. His thirst was strong, but not so strong he'd rush to take her.

No, he would enjoy her as he did every night he came to her. The soft creamy skin of her cheeks held a permanent tinge of rosy pink. One small freckle sat on the left side of the bridge of her nose. A slight amber highlight colored her perfectly cared for brown eyebrows.

She fished the keys from her pocket, squeezing the key

to the front entrance between her thumb and forefinger. One more deep breath, and she pushed open the door protecting her from the convenience mart's customers.

In the three weeks since he'd met her, he'd come to her more often than he should, drawn to her in the same way a child is drawn to a candy store. If he were being honest with himself, he'd have to admit it shocked him. Something about the woman drew him back, night after night. This was an experience he'd never had.

Inside the convenience mart he'd only seen her smile a very minor smile, one that indicated she was fine, but nothing more. A full smile never graced her lips, not until they were alone. To his surprise she also laughed, which made him happy. There'd never been a sound he enjoyed more.

Guilt jabbed into his brain. He shouldn't be here. He shouldn't come to her. It wasn't safe for her or fair. He never let her remember their time together, though there was nothing in the world he wanted more than for her to remember and to want more of those stolen moments. But he couldn't trust himself. He couldn't trust he wouldn't hurt her.

The pain in his chest flared. He shouldn't be here.

Something clattered within the convenience mart, and she swore out loud. Serge tried not to laugh. She wasn't the most coordinated woman he'd met. It was part of her charm.

Three nights ago he decided not to come, not to see

her. He couldn't. He needed to put distance between them. Safety was the reason. Hers, his, Central City's, The Vampire Guard's. He had plenty of reasons not to see the lovely gas station attendant.

But three nights had seemed like an eternity. An eternity of agony. This evening he'd managed to stay away long enough to allow the sun to set fully on the horizon before coming for gas, then back for batteries, then one of those odd fruity drinks, and then a box of sugar. If she hadn't looked at him like he was nuts the fourth time he went into the store he might have ended up with a kitchen full of stale groceries he'd never use.

Now he simply watched, enjoying the sight of her working. He could hardly wait to be alone with her behind the building. Those moments together had become his favorite time of night. His secret paradise. His time with her was a reprieve from the world with all his responsibilities, all the pain and danger. It was when he learned all about her day and her life and who she really was.

Devoted. Smart. Alluring. Inspiring. Sexy. Defiant.

Her chin held a small cleft, which she'd jutted out at him on several occasions. He believed she liked to think her obstinacy knew no bounds. Though, he'd proven her wrong every time for his persuasiveness could not be rivaled.

Serge grinned in spite of himself. One did not survive centuries by being denied.

Excerpt from

THE VAMPIRE'S PENANCE

ROMANCE IN CENTRAL CITY NOVELLA FIVE

Raffaele Valentino crashed onto the pavement, whacking his head hard enough to see stars.

"Are you crazy?" Garrison's arm locked around Rafe's chin. "You'll burn if you go out there."

"Get off me!" Rafe knocked him off his back, but the damn fool tackled him again.

The two men fell to the ground wrestling.

"You son of a bitch." Rafe planted his fist on the side of Garrison's head. "He's getting away."

"Which is what he wants!" Garrison yelled and took a shot at Rafe.

"Damn him!" Rafe was too late. He'd missed the only opportunity he'd get to stop his brother from making the stupidest decision of his life. He paced up to the edge of the building, remaining in the shadow, watching Gabe's car fade into the distance.

The black sun-deflecting windows made it impossible for anyone to catch a glimpse of Gabe, but Rafe knew his brother drove away smiling.

What was he thinking?

For the last several weeks, Gabe had been quiet. He spent most of his time on his damn phone, which was a complete shock to Rafe. In fact, he'd wondered if somehow Gabe hadn't become addicted to a ridiculous video game or if he hadn't become one of those idiots who had to constantly check his email or play on some social media site.

As it turned out, it was neither of those issues. Instead, only a few short hours ago Rafe found out he'd met a girl. On the Internet. In a chat room.

Gabe. His brother who had learned from him to trust no one, ever, about anything, for any reason except, of course, your brother.

For two hundred and fifty years it had been the two of them against the world. They'd traveled, caroused, fought, explored, and even on occasion shared women. But never had either of them gone off the deep end by running into the unknown, unprotected and unprepared for what could be waiting.

"He's making a huge mistake," Rafe said.

"Ah, don't be such a killjoy." Garrison stood beside him, keeping several inches between him and the sunlight.

"A killjoy?"

"Yeah, just because you don't want to find true love doesn't mean he doesn't."

Rafe glared at the idiot to his left. "He is chasing after a woman he's never met at one of the most dangerous times. We are being openly hunted and he's chasing women."

The idea of how stupid his brother was being made Rafe's head pound. Rafe had sworn an oath to protect him, and he'd done just that all these years.

"Trust me. Raymond Tyrone is not running a secret Internet dating service as a front to trap love-sick vampires." Garrison opened an app on his phone. "Though, an Internet dating service for vampires isn't a half bad idea."

"He's thinking with his dick." Rafe punched the brick wall beside him, putting a fist-sized hole in the mortar and sending cracks sprawling in every direction. "He'll get himself killed."

"Did it ever occur to you he might be running off to be with the love of his life? Maybe the woman he's meeting really is perfect for him." Garrison pulled out his phone and pointed it at Rafe.

"If you take one picture of me, I will shove that phone so far down your throat, you'll have pictures of the inside of your ass."

Garrison paused then pocketed the phone. "That is not a very nice way to talk to your partner."

Rafe didn't bother to hide his disdain for Garrison. He hadn't hidden it since the moment they'd met two years ago. He'd managed to avoid being stuck alone with the man everyone considered to be a pain in the ass for longer than a few minutes at a time. But now with Gabe gone and the order from the top that all vampires must be in pairs when on the street, he was stuck with The Vampire Guard's royal pain in the ass.

The phone in the inside pocket of his leather jacket vibrated. Without taking his glare from Garrison's face, he removed it. A picture of a nearly exact replica of himself shown on the screen.

Gabe. Same dark hair, same angry stare from deep gray eyes. Same tattoo on his neck. The only difference was Gabe's chin was clean-shaven in the picture. *To make sure you know it's me calling and not you calling yourself,* the little shit had explained when he gave Rafe the phone.

"What are you doing? Come home," Rafe said without waiting for a greeting from Gabe.

"I know you're worried, but I've got this. I'm not running into anything with my eyes closed. I know the dangers. Besides I'm strong, and my instincts are as sharp as yours." Gabe's voice sounded exactly like Rafe's. Everyone complained about it. Even vampires couldn't hear the one distinction between the two.

Gabe had a very slight lisp. He'd had it from the moment he learned to speak. Rafe spent several decades training him to speak without it. No one who didn't know ever heard it. But Rafe heard it. In his mind, Gabe would always be his baby brother, the one who needed protecting.

"You're arrogant," he said, using their native Italian so the town busybody who stood beside him listening with the intensity of a buzzard hovering above road kill wouldn't have any fodder for the gossip mill. "Arrogance leads to destruction."

Gabe laughed. "How's Garrison treating you?"

"It appears he may be dead by nightfall."

He laughed again. "I won't be gone long. Try not to do anything I wouldn't."

Rafe felt a smile threaten the corner of his mouth. Gabe and he had talked a number of times about what should be done to Garrison. They'd agreed to volunteer for the mission and had compared notes on exactly how they'd complete the task. Gabe's ideas were far more creative than the ones Rafe had devised.

"You do not know this woman," he said, returning to his primary concern.

"I do."

"No, you don't. You're being foolish. People you meet on the Internet are not your friends. They don't care about you. They will take advantage of you." Rafe knew he sounded like someone's old father, but he was right, and Gabe was behaving like a child. "Come home."

"For all these years we have never relaxed and enjoyed the times. This is a chance for me to meet someone who has not been drawn to me by vampire magnetism or because she thinks I can buy her something or because she believes I have the power to pull her out of that pit. This is cerebral. She hasn't even seen a picture of me."

"You sound pathetic." Rafe stepped away from Garrison. Watching his damn face while listening to Gabe was making him want to beat him dead. "Women fall all over you."

Women had been falling all over both of them from the moment they'd both become men. The vampire allure simply multiplied the effects. Getting a woman had never been an issue.

"Yes, but I want a woman to be my equal, not use me or…try to fuck her way into my life. I want to be with a woman I respect, one who respects herself and me."

Rafe flinched.

This was his fault. He'd raised Gabe and he'd turned him vampire, and then taught him how to be a vampire. He never taught him how to love a woman the right way. That was a lesson he'd been too afraid to teach.

"Come home. You can find a woman in Central City."

"I will be home. After I meet Aurelia." Gabe hung up.

Rafe stared at the phone in his hand, teetering between crushing it and hurling it. His hand shook with fury. Finally, he threw the phone as hard and far as he could into the open street, out into the sunlight.

Garrison whipped around, watching the phone sail out of the shadow. "Oh man, that was stupid."

"Ow!" a female voice shouted. "Who threw that?"

"I'll bet that hurt." Garrison rubbed his head. "Ever consider pro baseball? No, too many day games, right?" He laughed.

"We'll get my phone and then go inside to hide until nightfall," Rafe said.

Here he'd just lectured his brother on stupidity only to throw his phone out into the street for anyone to pick up. Information on everyone in The Guard was in that stupid device. He'd just put everyone at risk.

LOOK FOR THESE OTHER STORIES BY JORDAN

ROMANCE IN CENTRAL CITY NOVELLA SERIES

Her Vampire's Promise

The Vampire's Partner

A Vampire's Passion

His Vampire Past

The Vampire's Penance

The Vampire's Prophecy, April 2016

THE EVA PRIM SERIES

The Demon Mistress

Book One in The Eva Prim Series

Prim & Proper

Book Two in The Eva Prim Series

Coming June 2016…

The Road To Hell

Book Three in The Eva Prim Series

THE EVA PRIM SHORT STORY COLLECTION

Demons and Deep Dish Pizza

Demons and The Dark Roast

Choices. Anarchy. Hypocrisy.

ALSO AVAILABLE

Black Magic Rose

Book One in The Alliance

THESE BOOKS BY JORDAN ARE AVAILABLE IN PRINT

The Demon Mistress

Book One in The Eva Prim Series

Prim & Proper

Book Two in The Eva Prim Series

Black Magic Rose

Book One in The Alliance

FIND JORDAN'S BOOKS HERE:

Amazon: http://amzn.to/1ef3OsG

iBooks: http://apple.co/1AeJcuw

B/N: http://bit.ly/1AlfgwA

Kobo: http://bit.ly/1KjqqW0

Google: http://bit.ly/1K04Fr8

About Jordan

Jordan loves vampires. She also loves to laugh. And if you know anything about Jordan, you know her vampires will make you laugh.

A few years back Jordan received a copy of Twilight from her husband as part of her anniversary gift. By the end of that week she'd read the entire series and moved onto Anne Rice's Vampire Chronicles. Eight weeks and eighteen vampire books later the idea for her first book came to her followed very quickly by Eva Prim.

Having lived in Rhode Island for most of her life Jordan uses the state as a backdrop for all her books, though many of the cities and towns and businesses (especially the ones run by vampires) are all fictitious.

When she's not writing about one vampire or another Jordan enjoys spending time with her husband, Ken and their lovable Labradors, Dino and Enzo on the beautiful beaches of New England.

For more free books join Jordan's newsletter at http://bit.ly/1Vk2TWn

FIND JORDAN AT:

Find Jordan on her website at www.jordankrose.com.

Follow her tweets on http://bit.ly/1CmMPQk

Like her on Facebook at http://on.fb.me/1FUrNaX

Follow her Pinterest boards at: http://bit.ly/1J2iYJG

Friend her on Goodreads at: http://bit.ly/1CmN4ec

Google: http://bit.ly/1KKewFb

Amazon Author Page: http://amzn.to/1gll1lc

25292534R00087

Made in the USA
Columbia, SC
03 September 2018